Dedication

To those who knew the womb, but never the breath of life.

a novel

ONE LIFE

alvis west

ALDA
PUBLISHING
BAKERSFIELD
CALIFORNIA

Published by Alda Publishing, an imprint of Archer Ellison Publishing Company, Lake Mary, Florida

First printed in 2007

ISBN 10: 1-57472-325-1
ISBN 13: 978-1-57472-325-0

Printed in the United States of America

Cover design, Interior Design and Layout: Bookcovers.com

Contents

Chapter 1

Friends, Hero, and Mom

Life passes too quickly. One minute you are entering kindergarten and the next you are graduating from college and beginning an exciting career. Everything in between is just a blur of memories, moments, and minor monuments.

Let us, for a brief moment, consider one particular life. Euell Edwards came into this world at 10:03 P.M. on a cold, rainy night. He wasn't a huge baby by any stretch of the imagination. In fact, he weighed nine pounds and eight ounces and was measured as 22 inches long. But, he had the potential of being a big man. And, I do not mean necessarily big in height, breadth, or girth, for that matter. I mean that he had the potential to change the world. When I consider this idea, I guess we all have that potentiality. Maybe we don't recognize this fact early enough, or perhaps we allow daily life to get in the way of the things that are really significant for our earthly existence. Even more so is the neglect of that which has eternal significance.

Euell was born to a young mother who had become pregnant out of wedlock. She had considered the options many others in her situation had previously pondered. Should she keep her baby despite the fact that she had other plans that did not include another mouth to feed? Should she drop it off at someone's doorstep? Should she put it up for adoption? Or should she do as so many other women and have an abortion? Perhaps there was a solution that had not as yet presented itself.

Our story picks up sometime after that momentous decision was made. Euell was on his way to school. His first two weeks of seventh grade had not been too bad. In fact, he had made friends with John Easton after discovering that they had a number of things in common. One of these was softball.

"John! Wait up!" Yelled Euell when he saw his friend some distance ahead.

"Oh, hi Euell," replied John as he turned and waited for Euell to catch up with him.

"Did you catch the big game last night?" Euell inquired.

"I got to see most of it. But homework and chores got in the way. You know how it is at my house."

"Yeah. At mine too. But, I got to watch the game this time. My team won, of course."

"Don't rub it in," John replied in jest.

The boys reached the street crossing as the light changed from red to green. The girl just in front of the boys stepped into the street at the very moment that a speeding car came barreling toward the intersection. It was evident that the driver was not going to stop. As the car headed directly toward the girl, Euell ran and lunged as hard as he could. He hit the unsuspecting girl with a kind of high block that threw her clear of the car and plummeted her to the pavement with great force. As he stooped to pick her up, pandemonium broke loose. A police car was in pursuit of the reckless driver, siren, lights and all. A teacher, the principal, and a number of parents came running into the street to aid the two students. Everyone was talking at once. Euell asked the victim if she was all right. So did everyone else. All was a jumble of words-actually more of a cacophony than anything else. John, still standing at the curb, checked the traffic and joined Euell in the street.

"I thought you were both going to die!" he exclaimed excitedly.

"Yeah, so did I," replied Euell.

"Young man, come here please," interjected the principal.

"He was just trying to..." John managed to say before the principal cut him short.

"I know. I saw the whole thing. What's your name, young man?" the principal asked as he and Euell reached the sidewalk on the school side of the street.

"Euell," he replied somewhat sheepishly.

"And your last name?"

" Edwards."

"Well, Euell Edwards, you just saved a girl's life! Thanks

to you, all she has is a few scrapes and bruises. I have to say that what you did was heroic. Most people would just stand and watch out of fear, or some kind of inability to react. Come with me to the office so that we can write a full report and call your parents to let them know what happened." Turning away from Euell for a moment, the principal made a quick visual survey as to personnel. "Mrs. Johnson, will you take care of our injured girl and have someone call her parents? Turning back to Euell, he said, "Now Euell, I..."

The principal's conversation was interrupted by one of the office staff members holding the office door open. "Mr. Timberlane, officer Brant is on line three. It's about the incident."

"Thanks. I'll take the call in my office in a moment. What do you have first period, Euell?"

"English," he replied.

As they entered the office Principal Timberlane said, "Ask one of the secretaries to call your teacher to get you on the daily attendance record. We don't want you marked absent. And, I'll be with you in a few minutes."

John and the other students had to go on to class. As John entered the classroom his teacher met him at the door. "John, I've heard bits and pieces about what just happened. Some of the students said that you were there. Would you mind telling the class what happened so that we can dispel any rumors?"

John was usually very shy. But, on this occasion he found the courage to stand in front of the class and reveal the heroic actions of his best friend. Many of the students seemed surprised. One boy, obviously jealous of the attention said, "Anyone could have done what Euell did."

The teacher ignored the student's intent and generalized by saying, "But, the question is, would just about anyone put himself in harm's way for someone he didn't even know? I thank God that Euell was there at the right time and that he acted so bravely."

One of the girls in class raised her hand and asked, "Can we say 'God' in the classroom?"

The teacher replied quickly, "That depends on who you ask. I will not bother to ask permission from the ACLU. They would find my positive mention of God as harmful, offensive and antagonistic in some way!"

While the details and banter continued in the classroom, the young girl whose life was almost cut short was in the process of being washed and medicated as she eagerly awaited the arrival of her parents.

Principal Timberlane walked past the injured girl and flipped a switch on the intercom. The all-call seemed appropriate in light of the day's events. "Good morning, students, staff, and teachers. I'm sure that by now you have heard that we had a near tragedy this morning. But, thanks to our newest hero, Euell Edwards, a young girl was spared serious injury, or worse. When you see the victim and hero around campus, say hello."

Typical of a junior high school audience, some of the students expressed surprise. Some of them kind of blew it off. Others seemed somewhat nervous or even frightened by the story. Such an event seems to shake ones complacency and serves to remind all of the fragile nature of life, irrespective of ones age.

Euell's mother, Martha Edwards, had been called and had seemed reluctant to come to the school. She had not been told the reason for the request for her presence. All she knew was that there had been an incident of some kind involving Euell. As she entered the school office she saw her son seated in a chair near the principal's office.

"What has Euell done?" she inquired of the secretary standing nearby. "He has never been in trouble before. Has he been in a fight?"

"No. Nothing of that nature," replied Principal Timberlane as he stepped from his office. "A speeder almost hit one of our students. Your son pushed her out of the way and saved her from serious injury, or something much more serious. Your son is a hero. He put himself in harm's way to save someone he had never met."

Ms. Edwards turned her attention back to her son. Searching for words she asked, "Why? How? Why would you take a chance like that?"

The principal looked surprised. "If he had not done something we could be taking a student to the morgue instead of honoring Euell's bravery."

Ms. Edwards continued to look directly at Euell's bowed head. "You could have been hurt. You know that we do not have insurance for that kind of thing. Why didn't you think before getting involved in someone else's business?"

The principal and others had shock written all over their faces. And, Euell looked hurt, puzzled, and embarrassed. After a brief pause he said, "I didn't really have time to think. But, how could I have done anything else and lived with my conscience?"

Euell knew from experience that his mother would have much more to say to him in private once he got home.

Chapter 2

Plans and the Bible

The next couple of weeks were quite different for Euell and John. They continued to walk to school together. But, they received attention that they had not noticed previously, and they had a new friend of the feminine gender to accompany them to and from school. Her name was Mandy Lassiter. She and her parents had made it clear to Euell and his mother that they would be eternally thankful for Euell's unselfish actions that had preserved Mandy's health, and her very life. The local newspapers had even printed the story of the rescue, the community reaction to the heroics, and all the hoopla that had followed the event. Most of the community members were positive and supportive. But, of course there are always the nay-sayers.

The first few walks to school as a trinitarian group had been a bit awkward. Finally, Mandy admitted to the boys, "I really don't know how to talk to boys. What do you guys talk about?"

John was quick to state, "Softball or baseball!"

"Well, not *only* sports that we like. We also talk about

karate, school, music. You know. Things like that," Euell explained.

"Karate?" Mandy inquired. "Are you really interested in martial arts?"

"John and I are both interested. He can't take lessons because his parents are against the idea. I can't because I don't have the money."

"How much is it?" Many inquired.

"I really don't know. I just know that my mother said that we will never have the money for frivolous things like karate. I may try to earn money to pay for lessons by mowing lawns, washing windows, or something else. But, the truth is that school, homework, odd jobs, karate classes, practice at home, and softball may be too much for me to handle." Euell looked tired and frustrated as he thought about the hypothetical grueling schedule.

"My father knows a sensei quite well. He may give you a break on the price. I will ask Dad tonight."

"Well, Mandy, I would love to take a class. But, I don't know if it would work out. I don't mean just the money. I would feel a lot better if John could join when I do."

"I really don't know if I am the karate type," John said rather emphatically.

"Who is? I don't think anyone is born with all the skills. A person would have to *become* the type. And, Mandy, go ahead and ask your father about the sensei if you don't mind."

"Well, all right! I will," Mandy promised.

By that evening Euell had almost forgotten Mandy's promise. There were so many things on his mind, and the whole thing seemed like a pipe dream anyway. When Mandy called she told Euell that her father had called Sensei Brown minutes after she had made the request. The sensei had told her father that he needed someone to clean the dojo, set up equipment, put things away at the end of the sessions, and do odd jobs that he did not have time to do personally. The labor would cover the cost of the lessons. Furthermore, Mandy had asked her father if she could join the class as well. Surprisingly, he had agreed to pay for the lessons. Euell was so excited that he forgot to thank Mandy before he hung up the phone. He had to call her back quickly, thank her, and call John.

When he called John's residence, his father answered the phone. Euell told him that he and Mandy were going to begin karate lessons. "I would love to have John in the class with us. He and I have talked about how great it would be to learn this martial art and perhaps others. We will learn discipline, self defense, basics, basic movements, kata, and sparring. It should be a lot of fun and good exercise as well."

John's father said he would talk it over with his wife and John, and make a decision regarding the matter.

The days seemed terribly long as the three friends waited for an answer. Finally, early one morning, on the way to school, John seemed to be bursting at the seams. He finally exclaimed loudly, "Dad said yes!"

The three friends walked a bit faster that day as they made their way to first period. After second period they met and walked to third period history class. It was the only class the three shared. The current topic was ancient Egypt. Their teacher was an interesting man who had traveled extensively and who usually had lively, interactive classes. After the roll was taken, the pertinent historic quote from the board was discussed as a kind of springboard to the reading and question and answer session. A fifteen minute reading was assigned and then the question and answer segment was based on the fifteen minute reading as well and the homework from the previous evening.

The teacher asked, "Why was Egypt the Gift of the Nile?" One of the students answered the question by referring to the flooding of the Nile River and the resulting deposits of rich soil to the banks, and the shipping of goods up and down the river. Another student spoke about the drinking water for humans and animals and the irrigation of crops in a thirsty land.

"Question number two. Were the Egyptians polytheistic or monotheistic?"

Mandy quickly raised her hand and was called on. "Both," she replied. Student laughter followed. As she turned a bright red, she explained that the Egyptians were polytheistic throughout a great deal of their history. This actually changed when Akhnaton tried to replace the old system of worship with the worship of Aton, god of the sun disk. This religious reformer believed that Aton was the one and only god.

When class was over, Euell asked Mandy how she knew so much about religious things.

"Well, my father is a professor of ancient history and he tells us all kinds of things about the Babylonians, Assyrians, Egyptians, Hittites, Greeks, Romans and others."

"So he likes the social, political, and economic histories of the ancient cultures? Where does the religious aspect fit in?" Euell asked sincerely.

"My father says that all the aspects of a society are significant if one is to understand the culture. He also speaks at our church regarding the cultural baggage and the religions of the various civilizations as they are similar to, or distinct from, Christianity."

"So your family is religious?" asked John innocently.

"We are. We go to church every Sunday and sometimes on Wednesday. More importantly, we try to live like the Bible teaches. My father calls this the Christian world and life view."

Euell politely challenged the lifestyle Mandy had just pictured. "How can anyone do all the Bible says to do? I've read parts of it here and there and I can't imagine following all of those rules, and knowing all that religious stuff. It must be difficult studying in school all week long and then studying some more on Sunday."

"Well, it's not just on Sunday that we study the Bible. We do that every day. It is part of our lives. Actually, it is one of the most important parts. Without God we would be lost. And, I mean that in more than one way."

"What do you mean?" John asked.

Mandy, trying hard to say the right thing, finally replied, "We would be like a ship without a rudder. In the Gospel of John, chapter three, verse sixteen, we are told that God so loved the world that he gave his only begotten son so that who ever believes in him will have eternal life. This impacts all of life's direction."

"But, no one lives forever," John replied emphatically.

Euell nodded in agreement. "I have never known anyone to have lived forever. Where are the people from Jesus' day? They are all dead."

Mandy tried to be patient, and to give a thoughtful reply. Finally she gave a guarded reply. "Their bodies are dead. But, their eternal spirits live on in one of two places-Heaven or Hell. Would you two like to go to church with me sometime?"

John and Euell both agreed that they would give it a try sometime. And as they walked off toward their own homes they had time to ponder their growing friendship, the question of God and religion in general, and the expectation of the things each of them would experience and learn in the coming days as they began their lessons in the Japanese martial art called karate. Life can be good sometimes.

Chapter 3

The Dojo and the Bully

Euell arrived ten minutes early for his first assignment at Sensei Brown's dojo. The sensei (teacher) was a man of average build and height. But, Euell noticed that he walked with a definite air of confidence-without-arrogance. The sensei and Euell shook hands and introduced themselves.

Mr. Brown explained how to clean the equipment, where the cleaning materials were kept, how and when to clean the dojo, how to set up the kicking bags, and where to set the target gloves, portable kicking bags, and other pieces of equipment to enhance the martial arts training.

Euell caught on quickly and accomplished the assigned tasks much faster than Sensei Brown had anticipated.

"Do you have a ghee?" asked Sensei Brown.

"What's a ghee?" Euell inquired.

"It's the karate uniform that is designed for the kind of training we will be doing."

"Do I need one, and how expensive is it?"

"It is best that you wear one. This is especially true as you achieve rank. Wearing the traditional ghee makes you feel like part of the class. It is a reminder of the fact that karate originated in Japan and that we are carrying on their particular martial art tradition. If you don't wear the ghee you may ruin your street clothes. I will have to check on the price. But, I know that the brand we use recently increased in price."

"I will have to save some money until I can afford to buy one."

"Well, for now, you can borrow one. See the clothes rack to the left? You can use the ghee at the far end of the rack. I will find a white belt for you."

"Thanks. I really appreciate all that you are doing for me."

"No problem. Are you ready for your first lesson?"

"I hope so. My friends, John and Mandy are also starting lessons tonight. They signed up a couple of days ago."

"Good. I remember when they came in with their parents. Of course you know that Mandy's father, Dr. Lassiter, is a good friend of mine. We have known each other for a number of years. In fact, he has asked me to do karate demonstrations at university cultural events a number of times. I always agree. It's good PR and its good for my continued enrollment. In fact, getting college kids in class sets a good example for the younger students. Seldom are any of the college students the bully boy types. They are here to learn a skill. Well, you can change clothes and do some stretching exercises until the others arrive."

Euell changed into the ghee. The only problem was that he didn't know how to tie the belt properly. There was a picture on the wall that showed the desired result. But, there were no intermediate steps to follow in order to achieve the appropriate look. He was about to find the sensei to obtain the necessary help when several of the students entered the dressing room. One of them looked at Euell with a degree of recognition. He moved toward Euell and invaded his space. Leaning in close to his face, the young man asked, "Aren't you that seventh grade kid that I saw in the newspaper? The one that became an overnight hero-boy?"

"Well, I wouldn't call myself a hero. I was in the right place at the right time to do what needed to be done."

The young man took a step backward and looked Euell over from head to foot. "Hey guys. This hero-dude can't even tie his belt right!"

Laughter followed. Euell hadn't expected this kind of treatment. He was embarrassed and humiliated. The bully said disgustedly, "Here. Follow directions. I will tie my belt slowly. Do everything that I do. Imitate me. I will show you only one time."

The bully demonstrated in a condescending way. But, Euell followed carefully and accomplished the task correctly the first time. Regardless, the finished product didn't please Euell's antagonist. "Here. I'm going to untie this thing and tie it right! It's too loose!" He pulled the belt so tightly that Euell felt like he was being cut in half. The other students laughed.

Well, not all of them. Several of the older students shook their heads in disbelief. As Euell left the dressing room he saw one of the guys who hadn't appreciated the show walk over to the culprit and talk to him in hushed tones.

Euell noticed that many of the students had arrived dressed for class. He could understand why. No one wants to be humiliated by a bully. Some of the students were signing the attendance sheet. Others were paying the monthly fees. All of the experienced students were trying to stretch and to throw a few punches and kicks before the session formally began.

Mandy and John arrived in time to sign in and line up with the others when Sensei Brown gave the command. Of course the new students had lined up in the wrong positions. They didn't know about rank formation. The sensei patiently explained the rank line positioning and rearranged the class quickly. The class began with the traditional ceremony that involved bowing at particular intervals and from various positions. Each part was accomplished by the Japanese commands. The new students had to imitate those around them as best they could.

Sensei Brown called on the highest-ranking student to lead the formal exercises. The three abecedarians watched intently and imitated all the moves they were shown. The exercises were a mixture of those used in most any sport and those that seemed to be primarily pertinent to the physical moves involved in karate. Mandy, John, and Euell felt awkward and uncoordinated as they tried to follow each step with minute precision. And, they each knew that they looked foolish and clumsy.

After the rather rigorous workout, Sensei Brown stepped forward, bowed to the exercise leader, who reciprocated with an almost simultaneous bow, and took over the leadership of the class.

Sensei Brown addressed the class. "We have three new karate students with us tonight. Get to know them after class and help them get through the rough spots. All of you had some of the same difficulties when you first started. This first bit of instruction is not primarily for the experienced students. But, it does help you review the details of techniques and gives you the step-by-step procedural instruction you will be using when you teach various techniques to those who have not yet reached your rank. With this in mind, make a fist. Hold it up in a palm forward position so that I can see if the form is correct. I can tell from here that some of the more experienced students have gotten a little lazy or sloppy. The fist is not the weapon it should be. Open your hand. Curl your fingers tightly into a half fist as I am demonstrating. Curl your fingers a second time. This should result in a tight fist if your fingernails are trying to dig into the palm of your hand. Now take your thumb and place it at the second joint of the first finger like you see me doing. It will likely touch the middle finger slightly. Squeeze the fist as hard as you possibly can in order to make a rock solid weapon. The striking surface is not your whole fist. It is the first and second knuckle of the hand.

Striking with the other knuckles will likely result in injury to yourself. We minimize the striking area of the fist to maximize the power. That is, we put all the energy into two small points-the first and second knuckles. Watch as I align my two knuckles with an imaginary target. Notice that the angle of the fist and forearm are naturally out of alignment with the target. In other words, my third and fourth knuckles are going to strike the target. This has to be corrected. To accomplish the proper alignment, angle the fist downward slightly as to angle of the forearm. Next, turn the fist slightly toward the right side of your body if you are using the right hand, and toward the left side of your body if you are using the left hand. Each punch requires a slight bend in the elbow in order to avoid personal injury. Now, make both hands rock solid. Follow me as I count out the punches. Punch slowly as I punch slowly. That's not too bad. Let's increase the speed and power. Try not to move your shoulders."

After many awkward attempts the new white belt students were personally shown how to make the proper alignments and how to hold a proper stance for stability and maximum striking power. The bully green belt student was assigned the job of working with the beginners. The rest of the class worked out under the command of the sensei.

Mandy, John and Euell were doing well for beginners. But, the green belt began to watch Euell and nit pick every move he made. Yet, Euell was mature enough to make the best of a bad situation.

"The next step is the focused attack and response," Green-belt-bully stated as he stepped in front of Euell. "First, I want you to try to punch me in the solar plexus. That's right here under my sternum. Do this as hard and fast as you can. Try to knock the air out of me!"

Euell liked the idea. So he punched as hard and fast as he possible could. But, the bully blocked Euell's right arm with his left so hard that Euell was almost spun completely around. To add insult to injury, the bully-boy followed up with a right handed punch that landed hard on Euell's right shoulder.

"You two watch as we demonstrate this technique again." The greenbelt went through the full contact block and punch four more times.

When the formalities ended the class for the evening, Mandy, John, and Euell walked out tired and sore. Euell felt his swollen arm and shoulder. So this is karate. This would not be as easy as he had expected.

Chapter 4

Born Again

Mandy's open invitation to attend her church was eventually accepted. John and his family, Mandy and her family, and Euell sat together on the third row, listening to some of the songs and participating in others. John and his family seemed comfortable. But, Euell wasn't sure he was quite as comfortable. Perhaps it was because his mother had refused to come with him. In fact, she had scolded him for his plans. Euell could still hear his mother complaining, "Why would you waste a day in a church when you could be outside enjoying the real world?" Actually, he wasn't absolutely certain why this opportunity took priority over so many others. But, he was here none the less.

Euell listened to the actual words spoken in the church and paid attention to the things that were transpiring. He noticed that the minister prayed for the service, special needs of certain church members, the presence of the Holy Spirit, and for clarity in his sermon. These things intrigued Euell even though he did not understand what the presence of the Holy Spirit really meant. He would make it a point to ask Mandy after the service.

The pastor's message or sermon was taken from the third chapter of the Gospel of John. This seemed familiar in some way. Then Euell remembered that Mandy had occasionally quoted certain verses from this text. As the pastor read the passage Euell realized that there were words and names that he had never heard before. What was a Pharisee? Who was Nicodemus? What was a rabbi? What was the Kingdom of God? What was this thing about being born again?

Mandy and her family seemed to be following everything the minister was reading to the congregation. Euell glanced over at John and his family and drew the conclusion that they were as much in the dark as he was. But, things began to take on a new shape as the pastor explained each part of the passage in what he called expository preaching and exegetical analysis. It turned out that the Pharisees were a strict Jewish sect that prided themselves as keepers of the law and they believed in the resurrection of the dead. Nicodemus was a teacher, Pharisee, and member of the Sanhedrin or Jewish high court. He had come secretly to the rabbi (teacher) Jesus at night, to acknowledge God's working of miracles through Jesus. The messiah told Nicodemus that he had to be born again. The concept was foreign to this Pharisee. So Jesus explained that one must be born of water and the Spirit to enter God's kingdom. Eternal life in the kingdom was a future reality. Being a part of the kingdom not yet completed was a present reality. But, what was the water birth or the spirit birth? The pastor explained that the first birth is the water birth. The developing baby is carried in a fluid sack. The first birth is a precondition for the second birth. The second birth is by choice. It is made possible by the substitutional atonement of Jesus the Christ's crucifixion on the cross, in that all of man's sins were imputed to the suffering servant messiah. The plan of God is made complete in the individual when he or she believes on Jesus as the unique Son of God. Eternal life is through the Lamb of God. The pastor quoted John 3:16-the thesis statement of the Bible. Euell began to feel something he had never experienced before. Something was compelling him to respond in some way. But, how?

After the church service Euell asked Mandy and her parents what was actually meant by faith in Jesus and what he had to do to inherit eternal life. Each of them explained the experience from their own personal perspective and described what Euell would have to do. He would have to repent of his sins and personally accept Jesus' costly gift as the ultimate gift of grace. Immediately he understood experientially what he had only moments before begun to partially understand mentally. The Holy Spirit had directed him to the savior of the world. In that moment he became a new creation. His rejection by his mother was suddenly placed in juxtaposition with the unconditional love of God, and his new position as a son of God. Now he had a father. He was born of the Spirit, saved by the blood of the lamb, and forgiven for all his past, present, and future sins. Nothing in the world equaled this new relationship with his creator.

As Euell stepped out the front door of the church with Mandy, his antagonist happened to be walking by. Greenbelt said, "Hey hero! Are you trying to get God on your side? It won't help you at all if you show up for class next time!"

Euell didn't say anything in reply. He knew that he would have to learn how to live the Christian life in every circumstance.

Mandy finally asked, "What is his problem? He seemed to have it in for you the first night of karate."

"I'm not sure why he selected me as his personal punching bag. But, I think it has a lot to do with his self esteem and my pushing you out of the way of a speeding car. He called me the 'seventh grade's hero-boy' when I first met him in the locker room."

"Well, whatever it is, he's going to have to get over it! Do you want a ride home?"

"No thanks. John's family already offered. I'll see you tomorrow."

Mandy's parents had told the pastor about Euell's conversion. They stepped out of the church, found Mandy, and headed for home with complete joy over what had happened to the boy who had saved Mandy's life.

On the ride home, Euell talked incessantly about what he had experienced at church. But, he may as well have been speaking a foreign language. "This isn't going to be easy," he half whispered to himself.

Chapter 5

High School, Mom, and a Friendship Begun

Junior high school experiences faded as Mandy, John, and Euell entered the world of high school. They found that their time was full of activities centered on school, church, and karate. For Mandy and John, family time was factored in. For Euell there was no family life. But, his work at the dojo helped fill the time. And, it allowed him to continue taking lessons. But, Euell tried his best to avoid the green belt bully as much as possible. His failure to do so was visible via the bruises that were ever present.

On many occasions Euell talked with John about the salvation experience. He even talked with John's family members. But, they didn't seem to understand what he was talking about, nor why he spoke of it so often.

Euell's mother had been too busy and self absorbed to attend Euell's graduation from junior high school and she never attended his karate lessons, tournaments or softball games. It was obvious to everyone that Euell was an unwanted nuisance to his self-indulgent mother. Regardless of the situation and her attitude toward him, Euell tried to talk to her about things that were significant in his life. This meant trying to talk with her about spiritual things.

"Mom, why don't you go to church with me this Sunday and see for yourself what it is all about?"

"The church is full of hypocrites!" she replied forcefully.

"Well, so is the bar where you spend so much of your time. But, you still go there."

"I don't want any of that 'Holy Roller' stuff. It's for people who need a crutch."

"Alcohol is a crutch. And, do you actually think I need some kind of crutch? I have friends. I have softball and karate. I do well in school. Why would I need a crutch? God certainly is not a crutch. He's the answer to everyone's need to connect with the creator, savior, and sustainer of life!"

Ms. Edwards' anger was obvious. "That church has been filling your head with nonsense. The only life you will ever live is in the here and now. And, another thing. How can you call yourself a Christian and practice martial arts? Your Jesus was a pacifist!"

"From what I have studied, he was always eager for peace. But, he was not always pacifistic. He turned the tables on the moneychangers at the temple. He debated with the religious leaders of his day. One day he will judge the wicked. That does not sound like pacifism to me. Of course he was a pacifist when it came to converting the lost. He did not want to force anyone to accept him as lord and savior, and he did not want his apostles and other followers to use force. He used the marketplace of ideologies to convert the unbelievers. And, as far as karate, I will never use my skills to hurt someone without just cause. I certainly will not be a bully. The training gives me enough confidence that I don't have to fight in order to prove something. It keeps me physically fit. It gives my friends and me a chance to do something positive together. And, should the need ever arise, it gives me a fighting chance to save my life or that of someone else."

"Euell, you always disappoint me!"

"Why? Because I'm alive? You have never wanted me for your son. You don't take pride in my accomplishments in school, softball, karate, or church related activities. You seem to want me to disappear so you can live your life as though I never existed."

"Boy, you don't know the half of it! I wasn't married when I became pregnant. Your father and I married after I found out. But, that only lasted for a little over a year. He left me to raise you and support you. Neither of us ever wanted that responsibility."

Tears welled up in Euell's eyes as the enormity of his mother's words sank in. She had just audibly confirmed what he had always known to be true.

"Have I always been such a burden? I work for my karate lessons. My high school grades should enable me to get a college scholarship. Is my living that much of a burden on you?"

"You will find out when you have a child of your own. It is never easy. Everything has to be shared-your time, your money, your food, your house, and your future. Maybe the rich folks don't suffer through these things as much as we poor ones do."

"I don't think it has anything to do with how much money we have. What do you want me to do? Do you want me to make my own way, or perhaps pay your bills as well?"

"I really don't know. I don't know what to tell you."

Euell had a sick-all-over feeling and thought he would surely vomit before he could get to the bathroom sink. He had heard other people say that they did not think his mother loved and cared for him. He had always known in his heart that they were right. But, to actually hear his neglectful mother admit she did not even want him, hurt him as nothing on earth ever had.

Euell was feeling as low as a human could possibly feel, and knew that he had to get out of the house for a while. Perhaps a walk would help. As he walked, he began to think of a permanent change of venue. But, how could he survive? The few things in life that mattered would be gone. Well, some of them. He would still have friends even if they were physically distant. And, he would still have God!

The walk had taken him into a rather bad neighborhood. But, he was so deeply immersed in prayer that he had not noticed. By now Euell was unconsciously praying aloud. "Lord

God, please help me know what to do. You know all my hurts, needs, failures, and disappointments. Please help me!"

Just as he ended his audible prayer he saw Green Belt. Well, he was actually now a brown belt. Bully-boy yelled, "Hey! Hero! Are you praying that I don't bruise you all over again?"

Before Euell could even dignify the question with a response, three members of a local gang moved in on them with the obvious intent of doing them great bodily harm. One of the three said something about their turf and the fight was on. Bully- boy and Euell threw hard, fast kicks, punches, strikes and blocks as the street thugs kept attacking. Out of his peripheral vision, Euell saw Bully-boy knock one of the gang members out cold. Now it was two against two. Euell and his unlikely partner moved aggressively to end the fight. Finally, the gang members decided to give up the conflict, at least for the moment. Perhaps they were on their way to get reinforcements or weapons.

The two karate practitioners looked at each other and almost laughed out loud. Then Euell spoke. " My real name isn't really 'Hero-boy'. It's Euell."

"And, my name isn't Bully-boy. My name is Frank," replied the former bully.

A new day had dawned.

Chapter 6

Karate Progress and Three Guest Stooges

Karate class was not the same anymore. Actually that was a good thing. There was no longer the adversarial, antagonistic spirit that Frank had previously exhibited toward Euell. Frank's whole purpose was to immerse himself in karate. He read its history, watched karate movies, practiced the art many hours per day, and actually enjoyed helping other students learn speed, power, focus, timing, accuracy, forms (kata), sparring, and practical self-defense.

Euell not only enjoyed the change in Frank, he also enjoyed the assignments that came before the workout. It made him feel that he was learning responsibility, making his own way financially (to some extent), and helping others. The other students appreciated the attention to detail Euell brought to the job, and they understood that they were fortunate in that their parents paid for their karate classes while Euell had to pay for his own by the labor he performed.

While Euell was somewhat popular at school for his softball skills, his real love was karate. Mandy and John liked it, but Euell loved it. Their friendship with Euell kept John and

Mandy coming back for lessons and tournaments as each of them progressed through the ranks. In fact, when Euell made the rank of brown belt, he really blossomed. Frank, now a black belt, noticed the progress and helped Euell when he could.

"Euell, when you finish setting up the kicking bags I would like to help you with some advanced techniques."

"Sounds good to me," Euell replied excitedly as he quickly finished hanging the bags and putting various items in their places.

"I'm ready if you are," Euell said.

Frank stopped what he was doing for himself and crossed the room at a rather fast pace. As he reached Euell he threw a hard, fast, controlled punch at Euell's head. Euell barely blocked it in time.

"I wasn't ready for that one!" he exclaimed.

"I know you weren't. That's why I want to work with you on readiness, timing, and multiple responses or flurries."

For the next fifteen minutes the two practiced offensive and defensive counter moves. At times the sparring seemed almost choreographed. At other times Euell's Achilles heel was obviously exposed.

Mandy was a few minutes early for class and got a chance to see the two locked in combat. When they finished she exclaimed, "Wow! That was great! Euell, your sparring has really improved."

"Yes, it has improved a lot," Frank said. "He's learning to fight like a Chuck Norris or a Bill Wallace. He's not completely there yet. But, he's on the way."

After the other students arrived, signed in, and stretched, Sensei Brown formally started the class with the traditional bowing in ceremony. "There are a couple of tournaments coming next month. If you are interested you may want to check the bulletin board for all the details as to cost, location, and the kind of competition."

Sensei Brown divided the class into various levels. Frank took the green belt students. Another group was formed for the white belt level. The brown belt students were under Sensei Brown's instruction for the evening. Mandy, John, Euell, and four other students worked their way through a quick survey review of just about every technique they had ever learned. Next, they settled into a focused area that consisted of controlled, prescribed sparring. Limited contact was allowed.

The next segment required protective gear consisting of gloves for the hands and feet, headgear, and protective gear for the solar plexus, stomach and kidney areas. Other protective items of a personal nature were already being worn as a regularly prescribed precaution.

Sensei Brown said, "With the pads in place you can literally try to knock your partner out without any real danger of severe injury. But, do not put that kind of power into anyone's knee. And, remember we are here to enable each other, not to disable each other. An injured partner is an absent partner.

An absent partner leaves you no one to spar with. Rotating lines across from each other! Ready! Kumite!"

The sparring began in earnest. The brown belt skills were obvious, as the techniques were fast, furious, controlled, crisp, on target, repetitive, varied, and effective. Unfortunately the sparring was cut short by a sudden intrusion. Through the door came three bully-boy types with liquor on their lips and trouble on their minds.

The leader stepped onto the workout floor and announced, "This karate crap doesn't work. I'll prove it by taking on your toughest man, or woman, for that matter."

Sensei Brown stepped forward and politely, softly replied, "I have a class to teach right now. You can sit and watch if you wish. But, we have nothing to prove to you."

The loud mouth leader threw a wild, right-handed, hay-maker punch toward the sensei's head. Sensei simply responded with an upper/rising block with the left arm, an open palm strike with the right hand making ferocious impact under the aggressor's chin, and a jump kick to the assailant's chest. The knife-edge of the sensei's left heel had hit the sternum with enough force that the man had gone down hard and had struck his head on the floor. He lay there silently and didn't move at all. His friends realized that he was unconscious, and decided that a rapid retreat out the front door was appropriate.

Sensei Brown said matter-of-factly, "I'm sorry for the un-planned lesson in self defense. But, as you can see, too much confidence mixed with liquor can get you hurt. Another lesson we can learn is that if you take out the big mouth, the others will run like frightened rabbits. I need to call the police department for an officer to come and make a report. A couple of you should really stay to give your statements. Otherwise, class dismissed."

Chapter 7

Moving On and the Blues

Euell and his best friends tested for Shodan-Ho, the initial black belt ranking. Each passed with flying colors. At the presentation of rank certification were family members and friends from school and church. The one glaring exception was Euell's mother. She had told Euell that she would be busy that evening. Nothing had really changed. She had never watched his training sessions or his tournaments. So why did he expect her to come to an awards assembly and demonstration?

The ceremony was brief. Sensei Brown and the other black belts were up front. The ceremony opened with the usual bowing and customs of the martial arts. Sensei Brown welcomed the audience to the dojo and made some opening remarks. Frank read the name and new rank for each student and included a brief statement about the character and skill of each one. Sensei Brown handed out the certificates of rank and shook hands with each one as he or she walked across a temporary stage.

The guests were invited to stay for the evening's lesson.

Those who chose to stay were treated to a phenomenal experience as those who had been promoted, and those who had not, put on an impressive demonstration of the art of karate.

At the end of the evening, John, Euell, and Mandy talked with Sensei Brown about their plans. Each of them planned to cut back to working out twice a week in order to take on some other interests. Sensei Brown said that he would love to have them teach some of the sessions.

"Well," Euell began somewhat reflectively, once he was alone with his friends. "It has been quite a ride."

John and Mandy nodded in agreement. Mandy said, "I've signed up for archery. I don't know why I waited so long to begin. It is something I have had an interest in since I was six or seven years old."

"I will be enrolling in the judo school next week," John stated excitedly. "The school will be adding Ju Jitsu lessons next month. Who knows? I may take both."

"Not bad for a guy who didn't know if he was the karate type," Euell said jokingly. "I'm set to begin guitar and saxophone lessons sometime next week. I will try to find a part time job to pay for the lessons and rent or buy used instruments."

The Lassiters and Eastons decided to go out for a meal at a local Asian restaurant, and they invited Euell. "It's our treat," stated a smiling Dr. Lassiter. When he perceived that Euell was about to decline the invitation he said, "I insist!"

The group of friends discussed one topic after another over dinner. One of the big topics was college. Which colleges were best? Which subjects were the most interesting? Which major was best for each of them? What were their career goals? Although the answers to each of the questions were tentative, the discussion was a good starting point. And, Mandy, John, and Euell all agreed that it was likely that they would receive scholarships. The world full of choices and opportunities would be made day by day and experience by experience.

Like all things in life, the receiving of black belt rank, and the meal among friends gradually became a somewhat distant memory. As in all areas of life, it just kind of faded like one scene in a movie to another. The high school experience was about to do the same. Each of the three friends had indeed earned grades sufficient to receive scholarships. The emotionally negative side of this was that each of the college bound students had been selected by different colleges. They knew that this would mean a separation of four long years or more.

Euell knew that he would have to quit his job at the hardware store and prepare for the move to a place near the college. The hardware store owner had been nice enough to hire Euell at a time that he desperately needed work. This was soon after Euell had made the rank of Shodan-Ho and had begun lessons in guitar and saxophone. During this time Euell had continued to play softball, take karate lessons until he and his friends had reached Shodan (First degree black belt), and he had made time to clean the dojo as a favor to Sensei Brown.

This was true even on nights that he was not participating in either practice or instruction.

Mandy told John and Euell some news they had not anticipated. "My father surprised me last night. It turns out that he and mom have been planning this for some time. My family and I are going on a vacation to Europe and won't be back until near the end of summer break. Here is my college address. Will you both write me when I get settled in at school?"

Both boys agreed that they would write regularly. John said, "My family is going on a two week camping trip, and a number of excursions of two or three days duration off and on all summer.

As one could predict, Euell was not going on a vacation of any kind. In three days he was going to settle somewhere near the college campus, even if it meant camping out. He had enough money saved to get to his destination and to afford food and other necessities, if he was extremely frugal.

All three of the college bound students talked at length about their lives, memorable moments, inspiring teachers, classes together, and the way they first met. The conversation was understandably bittersweet. Each of them was eager to go to college, and they agreed that the high school experience had been more social for most students than it had been educational. They also agreed that too many kids left high school with a lifetime self image based on how popular they were during the high school years. For some this would be a good thing. For others, it would be a painful thorn in the flesh the rest of their lives. College should be a welcome change. After all, wasn't this where academic pursuits prevailed over social status? The goal for each of them was to immerse themselves in a world of learning.

Euell said, "I press toward the mark for the prize of the high calling of God in Christ Jesus. Philippians 3:14." Mandy nodded agreement. John just kind of stood there quietly with a sad look on his face.

The three friends embraced and said their good-byes. Each was teary-eyed as they walked away not knowing what the future held or whether they would see each other again. All they knew was that each of them had the best of intentions as to keeping in touch and maintaining friendships while, at the same getting a higher education.

As their distance from each other increased, there seemed to be a diminishing of the usual sounds of the birds chirping, and of the dogs barking. There was also a very real feeling that they were leaving the comfort of close friendships carved out of an often cold, callused, heartless world.

Chapter 8

Alone and Comfort Found

Euell was as alone in the world as he had ever been since that rainy night designated as his birth night. He was completely alone in a strange city. A Good Samaritan had allowed him camping privileges on his acreage situated just outside of the city limits. Euell had selected a semi-secluded, semi-protected area situated in a small grove of trees.

As Euell set up his one-man tent and situated his sleeping bag and other meager belongings, his mind kept focusing on his friends. John and his family were on a fishing trip. Mandy and her family were somewhere in Europe. His mother was doing whatever she usually did without having to bother with Euell. She wouldn't miss him for a second. These thoughts made him sad and lonely, but he had to think the thoughts to feel somehow closer to each of his people. Jealousy did not factor into the equation in any way, shape, form, or fashion. He wished for each one of them a world of health and happiness.

In less than three months Euell would be able to obtain a campus dorm room. Until then he planned to map out a strategy that would work for the immediate summer and the next four years or more.

Euell set up a small battery powered lantern that cast enough of a glow to allow reading. He looked at travel brochures pertaining to the area, and maps of the surrounding community. Once his mind was saturated with a basic orientation he decided to do some Bible studies. What did the Bible have to say about comfort? Euell used his concordance to find some answers. Psalm 23 looked like a good place to begin. He read aloud, "The Lord is my shepherd; I shall not want. He maketh me to lie down in green pastures: he leadeth me beside the still waters. He restoreth my soul: he leadeth me in the paths of righteousness for his name's sake. Yea though I walk through the valley of the shadow of death, I will fear no evil: for thou art with me; thy rod and thy staff they comfort me. Thou preparest a table before me in the presence of mine enemies: thou anointest my head with oil; my cup runneth over. Surely goodness and mercy shall follow me all the days of my life: and I will dwell in the house of the Lord for ever."

For quite some time Euell reflected on the meaning of that which he had read aloud and its application to his situation. It's significance fed his heart and mind and began to calm his spirit. It was the first time in some time that he had felt this close to God.

As he set the Bible down and turned over onto his back, his head was sufficiently outside the tent to see the stars in the night sky. He felt loved, accepted, protected, and in the company of the one who had created him and all the seen and unseen around him and in the heavens.

Euell turned back onto his stomach, retrieved his Bible, and read a Psalm of David that was a prayer for guidance and protection. He read the 25th Psalm slowly, deliberately and in such a fashion as to experience the feelings David had traveled through. Next, he scanned the other chapters in the Psalms. Chapter 22 caught his eye. He read aloud, "My God, why hast thou forsaken me?" He recalled that Jesus had spoken these words from the cross, perhaps as a messianic claim to the fulfillment of prophesy, perhaps to audibly signify the moment the full weight of man's past, present, and future sins were placed on his shoulders, or perhaps because neither Father God, the Son of God, the Holy Spirit, or the angels of heaven were to intervene in man's attempt to silence the way, the truth, and the life. Euell's thoughts turned to Pontius Pilot who asked Jesus," What is truth?" Pilot did not even know the truth when it was personified and standing in front of him looking him right in the eyes.

The pursuit of pertinent scriptures continued. Comfort was to be found throughout the Bible in the Old Testament and in the New Testament. So he turned to the latter. In the fifth chapter of Matthew Euell found the Sermon on the Mount. The Beatitudes were of great comfort. The fourth verse said, "Blessed are they that mourn: for they shall be comforted." He knew that his lifelong mourning was due to not having a father figure in his life and not having a mother who loved and cherished him as a mother should by nature, and by nature's God. Euell was at this moment receiving God's comfort. He looked up every biblical reference to the word "comfort" he could find. He looked up references to "comforter." All of God's inscripturated comfort pointed to the living God that cares for his creatures and does not leave them alone.

The Bible was put away, the lamp was turned off, and Euell settled in for the night. It did not take long for him to fall asleep. All night long he dreamed of God's comfort, love and providential grace. He also dreamed of his friends-especially Mandy. Suddenly his dream world revealed subconscious romantic feelings for her that he had never really considered previously.

Chapter 9

Food, Friends, and Goals

The next morning Euell awoke at the break of day feeling rested and a little stiff from sleeping on the hard ground. He used wet-nap towellettes to bathe and then he quickly brushed his teeth, combed his hair, shaved, and dressed for the day. Not knowing how safe his meager belongings would be if left unattended, he stuffed everything into his large backpack and headed down the road. He estimated that it was about a mile and a half to a small restaurant he had seen the day before. His walk was rather brisk in order to be one of the first customers of the day. But, when he arrived, the restaurant had not yet opened for business. A wooden bench just outside the front window became his waiting spot. As he sat drinking in his surroundings, he noticed that the sights, smells, sounds, and feeling tone of this community were quite distinct from home. Of course he was judging the whole community from one small segment. Maybe the differences weren't necessarily a bad thing. Distinctives are a part of life and a means of cataloging people, places, things, events, and ideas. They prevent life from being too mundane.

The wait wasn't too long. A middle-aged woman said hello to Euell as she unlocked the door and invited him in. "Have you been waiting long?" she asked.

"No, not really. I was kind of enjoying the scenery as I waited."

Before Euell could take a seat, other customers were pulling up and parking. A rather large man walked in and said hello to the waitress as he proceeded to go behind the counter and into the kitchen. Euell had already pegged him as the cook.

The money would be tight until Euell could get a job, do odd jobs here and there, or begin receiving the scholarship money. With this in mind, he ordered an orange juice and a bagel.

The waitress responded to his order with, "Honey, you must be hungrier than that!"

"No. That's all I need. Thanks," replied Euell sheepishly.

As more people came in, found seats, ordered and began to talk, Euell overheard a couple of men discussing the new Christian college and seminary that had just opened with the summer session. One of the men looked and sounded like a professor. The other was very articulate as well. But, he seemed to have some other kind of career.

Euell finished his meager meal, paid the waitress, and made his way to the table where the discussion of the new school was still underway. "Hello, I'm Euell Edwards. I don't mean to interrupt your conversation. But, I couldn't help but hear you mention a new Christian college and seminary. May I join you?"

"Yes, by all means. I'm Dr. Edward Cunningham, professor of New Testament Studies and Systematic Theology. And this is my literary friend, Bill Brighton."

After shaking hands, Euell sat down next to Mr. Brighton, who was moving over to make enough space.

"I'm here on a full scholarship to the university. My plan is to carry a full load of fifteen to eighteen units per term. But, I would be very interested in the Christian college and, perhaps later, the seminary. Would it be possible to enroll in one class at the college? Perhaps an evening class?"

"Well, young man, if you plan to carry that many units at the university you are not likely to have the time, nor the energy, to do more than the typical studying, doing research, doing the readings for each class, and preparing for exams. I seriously doubt that you will have time to take a class from another institution."

"I agree with Dr. Cunningham," Mr. Brighton said matter-of-factly.

"I think I could handle it. I've carried a heavy load consisting of classes, homework, a part time job, martial arts, softball, music lessons, church and time with friends. How much would one class cost?"

Dr. Cunningham replied, "I have a rough idea of the cost, plus books. But, it would be best if you spoke to our admissions and records office to obtain an exact dollar amount and information as to enrollment requirements."

"I assume that you are a Christian," Bill interjected.

"Yes, I am," Euell stated with conviction. "The first time I had ever been to church for anything but a wedding or funeral was with my best friends and their families. I was in junior high school at the time. When I heard the gospel I responded. I have tried to live the Christian life ever since."

Professor Cunningham frowned as though he didn't really know quite how he should phrase the next question. Then his eyes focused on Euell intently. "What are your educational goals and long term career goals?"

Euell responded immediately. "I hope to finish college and go on to graduate school for a masters degree and possibly a doctorate. I haven't decided which disciplines or which careers. I thought that the first two years of college would introduce me to enough subjects to allow me to make up my mind. I have a definite interest in law, ministry, history, literature, theology, medicine, missions, music and writing. The actual choice will be God's. I want him to lead me in all my decisions so that I am in God's will and working for his glory. For example, if I become a lawyer, I want to work for one of the law firms that defends Christian rights in our courts so that I can fight the godless, mindless, heartless onslaught perpetrated by groups such as the American Civil Liberties Union. Actually, I call this hate group the Anti-Christian Lawyers Union. There are several firms that I would consider. Among them are the

American Center for Law and Justice, the Rutherford Institute, the Alliance Defense Fund, Liberty Council, and the Thomas More Law Center."

"Those are honorable goals," Mr. Brighton said. "But, I agree with Dr. Cunningham that the work load will be horrendous."

"In junior high school I worked cleaning and doing set up for a karate dojo in order to be able to take lessons. And, I did the kinds of things I mentioned before. I have been an independent person who has been forced to fight for everything I've ever had. This will be nothing new."

"Sounds like you have been a very busy, determined young man," commented Mr. Brighton.

"Are you going to be forced to work while attending the university?" inquired Dr. Cunningham.

"Not as an undergraduate. My scholarship will cover everything that's essential. But, I could use some work this summer."

The professor sat quietly for a few minutes. Finally he asked, "How will you pay for classes at the Christian college?"

The response was immediate. "I would schedule some work time for after university classes and before the Christian college class. I know that I will have to study late into the night, between classes through the week, all day Saturday and some times on Sunday, after church."

"What about your many interests and activities?" inquired Mr. Brighton. Would these things get in the way of your studies?"

"I really don't know what I'll do about softball, karate, saxophone, or guitar. I guess I will have to put them on a back burner for now."

"Perhaps your part time job could be one in which you give lessons in karate or softball, guitar or saxophone. This would allow you to continue in things you enjoy and get paid for it as well," suggested Mr. Brighton as Dr. Cunningham nodded in agreement.

"Well, that's an idea that I will explore," Euell promised.

Dr. Cunningham stood and put his hand out to Euell. As the two shook hands, he said, "Well, it has been a pleasure talking with you, Euell. I want to wish you well, and I hope to see you on our new campus. Here's my card if I can be of any assistance."

Mr. Brighton dropped a tip onto the table and shook Euell's hand. "I'm glad you overheard our conversation and that we met. I wish you all the very best."

As Euell started to exit behind the two men, he spotted a day old newspaper and asked the waitress if he could have it. Permission was granted and he decided to sit back down and read for a few minutes. His attention was drawn to an article about one of the recent university graduates who had received his Ph.D. in political science, and had been offered a job at a well known university one week after having gone through the graduation ceremony. He was so excited about the possibility of getting started in a career immediately after graduation from college that he couldn't help saying aloud, "That's what I want!"

The rest of the day was spent walking around the town getting acquainted with the lay of the land, and the various buildings and businesses.

All in all, it was a nice community and a productive day.

Chapter 10

Nuts and Bolts, Scriptures and Realization

Euell set up his tent and few belongings quickly so that he could snack on some trail mix while writing letters to Mandy, John, Frank, Sensei Brown, and Euell's mother. He knew that Mandy wouldn't even see his letter until summer's end. But, it made him feel some way closer to her by writing. Besides, he was providing her a chronological account of his new life. John would probably read his letter after his family trip. Frank would be surprised. So would Sensei Brown. Euell's mother may not even read the letter.

Each letter shared some things in common while having their own distinctive qualities as well. The adventures were shared, but so too were the expressions of friendship and the longing to see each one. Once the letters were written, addressed and stamped, he realized that he had no return address to provide them. Hopefully, that would soon change.

Prayer and Bible study were next on the agenda. Euell prayed that God would protect his mother and his friends, and that they would prosper according to God's will and grace. He also prayed for forgiveness and gave thanks for the blessings of life. Before the "Amen," came an earnest plea for a heart and mind that was open to the Scriptures.

As Euell turned to the Gospel of John he decided to read aloud, take notes, and try to remember the commentary his hometown pastor had made relative to this passage and other, similar passages.

In the still of the night he read aloud, "In the beginning was the Word, and the Word was with God, and the Word was God. The same was in the beginning with God. All things were made by him; and without him was not anything made that was made. In him was life; and the life was the light of men. And the light shineth in darkness; and the darkness comprehended it not."

As he read the scriptures a second time, silently this time, he began to remember some of the commentary he had heard previously. Logic and context were tools he applied to the verses as to meanings and application to life. He wrote, "In the beginning," and made notes that this could not be a reference to Jesus' beginning. It must mean the beginning of the created order. The "Word" referred to Jesus and that fact that he had created all that existed by speaking all things into existence. Things began to exist because Jesus wished them to exist, and to continue to exist. The "Word" was with the father, Yahweh, and was God every bit as much as was Father God. Jesus was thus preexistent to the incarnation and to creation itself. Everything was created ex nihilo (out of nothing). It was not a rearranging of atomic particles. It was not a remodeling job. It was the creation of the very particles that would compose all forms of life and matter. And, in the creator was life itself, and the light for man's path. The light of ultimate truth shone in the darkness of nothingness and the darkness could not overpower or prevent it.

Though the verses were rather philosophically and theologically stated, Euell could recall enough of the preacher's commentary to complete the ideas essential to an understanding of the text. But, Euell wanted to be able to do so much more. That would take time, effort, and a formal education. And, for Euell, it wasn't knowledge for its own sake. William Patterson had expressed the idea so succinctly when he said, "The beauty of all knowledge consists in the application." For Euell, the application of scripture was personal first, and for the purpose of evangelical application second.

After the study of the scriptures Euell wished he had a small battery-powered radio. And, though he had never spent much time in front of a television, even it would have offered him some company. Hearing other human voices would have been nice. Eventually, after he got settled in somewhere, he would send for his saxophone and guitar. This would keep him occupied, and in practice.

As the tired pilgrim lay thinking of the past, the present, and the future possibilities, he placed Mandy into the framework. There was the past with Mandy as one of his best friends. There was the present with Mandy as geographically distant and as one to which to write regularly. There was the germination of thoughts about a future with her. But, what if John had similar latently revealed feelings for her? What if Euell was just lonely and putting too much stock in a dream? What if Mandy were to meet someone at the university or from her new community? The short separation from her had the benefit of raising questions and providing time, for a while anyway, to ask the right questions and to answer many of them.

As Euell pondered these things he became rather melancholic. A seemingly endless agony surfaced within Euell, as it had regularly since childhood. This was centered on, and caused mainly by, his mother's lack of love for him. It was also due to the knowledge that whatever he accomplished in life would never impress her or cause her to say, "I'm so proud of you for all you are, and all that you have done with your life." John's parents were vocal about his accomplishments. So were Mandy's. But, when you come down to it, "Life is made up of marble and mud." Nathaniel Hawthorne must have experienced a life similar to Euell's. How else could he have penned such insightful feelings as he had in the classic book, *The House of the Seven Gables*?

There must have been precious moments long forgotten in which Ms. Edwards had stayed home with Euell, enjoyed long conversations with him; taken him on long walks through the neighborhood; made him feel good about himself; spoken of her dreams and plans for the future; talked about Euell's father, what her parents were like, how she settled in this community, what she thought about the deeper meaning of life, why she didn't bring guests into their home, her favorite book, the music she enjoyed, the reason she hated Christians, and so much more. But, for the very life of him, Euell could not remember even one. Perhaps the problem was his memory. Was his memory selective? Did he have a mental block of some kind? Was he really less significant that all of the other people he knew?

Some answers don't come easily, and neither did sleep this particular night as he kept replaying negative life experiences, and trying to make sense of them individually or corporately. Euell tossed and turned, sat up to the extent allowed by the small tent, got out of the sleeping bag and went for a walk, watched the stars for awhile, thought of his favorite places on earth and how it would be to live in any one of them, and tried to visualize his life four years in the future.

As Euell rearranged his bedding and climbed back in, he felt compelled to pray once more. "Lord God, help me to really understand life and all the things I need to understand in order to please you. Make me a useful person for your glory and for my fellow man's need. May I always stay close to you and allow you to lead me through the mountains and through the valleys. Give me wisdom, knowledge, understanding, and application. May I be able to lead the atheists, skeptics, agnostics, secular humanists, and those of non-Christian religions to your truths. Bless and protect my mother and friends. Forgive me for my sins. Thank you for all past, present and future blessings. In Jesus' name I pray. Amen."

Restful sleep finally overpowered Euell's doubts and fears.

Chapter 11

The Law, New Transportation, and Dojo Hopping

Three forty-two in the morning was not what this vaga-bond had in mind for his wake up call. None-the-less, he was startled awake by the definite sounds of a person approaching his small tent. The crunching sound of boots on small limbs and brush not only awakened him from REM sleep, but also elevated his blood pressure considerably.

Euell started to ease out of the sleeping bag and prepare for a possible battle. But, before he could clear the bag a man's voice rang out. "Stay where you are! Do not move a muscle."

Immediately a flashlight was on and shining directly in Euell's eyes. "What are you doing here boy?"

Euell managed a shaky reply, "Trying to sleep. Who wants to know?"

"Don't be a wise guy young man! Again I'll ask you. What are you doing here?"

"I'm camping. Just trying to sleep."

"Who told you that it was all right to stay on this property?"

"Well…the owner, Mr. Barton. He said that I can stay here until I find something else."

"That's strange. He has never done that sort of thing before, that I know of. Do you have any proof?"

"You can ask him."

"Now, I'm not about to go waking a man up this time of the night to ask a question that I already know the answer to. What's your name?"

"Euell Edwards."

"Do you have any identification?"

"You still haven't told me who you are."

"I'll move a little closer so that you can see who I am." As he moved closer the light was still directly in Euell's eyes. But, he could see that the man was wearing a lawman's uniform.

Euell explained, "You really had me worried. Here is my wallet with a couple of forms of identification."

The lawman took the wallet, looked at the identification and said, "Stay here."

Footsteps moved away from the tent and a car door screeched open. Euell could hear bits and pieces of the conversation as the radio communication was transpiring. A few minutes later the lawman returned and tossed Euell's wallet onto the sleeping bag.

"Nothing on you, it seems. I'll talk with Ed after daylight. I copied down information from your identification cards. If there are any problems, or if Mr. Barton doesn't back up your story, I'll come looking for you. Sleep tight."

"Goodnight," Euell managed to say rather sheepishly.

Once the aroused sleeper's heart rate had come back down to normal, he began to relax and attempted to return to dreamland. When the sun came up, so did Euell. He went through the same ritual of preparation as he had the previous morning in order to quickly begin his trek to the restaurant. His sleep may have been aborted by a lawman first, and next by the morning sun, but his hunger had not.

As Euell passed Mr. Barton's house he heard someone call out, "Hey! Young man!" Euell turned in time to see Mr. Barton step from the porch and make his way toward him.

"I hear the law paid you a visit last night."

"Yes, it did. Frankly, I didn't know who it was or what he wanted at first. He kept a distance and had his flashlight shining directly into my eyes."

"He was just being cautious and looking out for me. I vouched for you. You can stay on my land as we agreed." That said, he turned and walked back to his house.

Euell again set out for the restaurant. In route, he mailed the letters he had written the evening before. When he arrived at the restaurant it was not yet open for business. He sat down on the wooden bench, pulled the two-day-old paper from his backpack and began to read various things of interest. When he started reading the want ad section he suddenly had an idea. He needed transportation, but lacked the funds for a car. What about a bicycle? There were several exotic racing bikes listed. But, they were too rich for his blood. Two listings for three speed bikes caught his attention. One was listed at ten dollars, and the other for twelve dollars.

The waitress and cook arrived simultaneously. Both said, "Good morning" and Euell replied in kind.

As Euell took a seat at the counter he asked the waitress, "Would you mind if I use your phone after I eat? I need to check on some transportation."

The waitress replied, "I don't mind at all, as long as it is a local call. I have a friend who is selling a nice car. I'll give you his number."

"Thanks. But, a bike is more my price range for now."

Euell ordered a small breakfast and continued reading the want ads. After eating he asked for the telephone. It was handed over the counter, and he called about the ten-dollar bike. The seller gave him directions to the house.

Euell followed the directions from the sloppy map he had scrawled hurriedly onto the backside of his receipt from the restaurant. He found the house without much difficulty. When he knocked on the door a retired gentleman opened it almost immediately. He was a pleasant looking man with a wide grin. "You're here for the bicycle?" he inquired.

"Yes, I am. I'm Euell Edwards."

"Glad to meet you. Follow me around back," he said, as he

stepped out the front door and headed toward the side of the house.

In the back yard was a nice storage shed with windows and carriage doors. The unit was filled with gardening supplies and yard tools. "There she is," the gentleman said proudly.

Euell was surprised at the almost new condition of the obviously old bicycle. It was dusty, but that would be an easy fix.

"Can I take it for a test run?" asked Euell.

"Of course. Just leave your backpack here and take her for a spin."

The bike rode well, shifted well, and seemed very appropriate for Euell's transportation needs. He rode the bike two blocks and returned. As he walked the bike into the back yard, he said, "I'll take it!"

The transaction having been completed, Euell was on his way, backpack on his back, ten dollars lighter, and two wheels wealthier. The bicycle would allow for faster transportation from place to place, and would be very helpful at the university.

When Euell saw a nice park off to his left, he decided to stop long enough to look at the job opportunities listed in the newspaper that he still carried in his backpack. After looking long and hard, he could find nothing in the way of an opening for a softball coach, karate instructor, hardware salesman, or custodian. He did not even bother looking for openings teaching guitar or saxophone, or for a band in need of his musical skills. Anyway, his instruments were still at home for now.

The next step required going directly to karate studios and seeking employment personally. If that did not pan out he would try various youth organizations that had sports programs in his areas of expertise, and talk with various managers at hardware stores.

On his way to the first karate school he had looked up in the phone directory, he saw a bike shop and stopped to purchase a locking bike chain. When he arrived at the first dojo he was disappointed that they had nothing for him unless he was willing to practice with the classes for free for a few months, or until the people got to know him well enough to consider hiring him. The second dojo visit turned out essentially the same way. When Euell entered dojo number three he was rather pessimistic. His lack of optimism became more acute after speaking with the head sensei. There were no openings. But, one of the students who had overheard the conversation stopped him as he was leaving and told him that the youth center on Seventh Street needed a self-defense instructor and perhaps a karate instructor. What did Euell have to lose besides a little time and some calories expended in the ride?

Chapter 12

Youth Center, Christian College, and
Promises

T he Community Youth Center was in an older building. But, it had been well maintained. Euell parked his bike in the bicycle area, locked it to the holder, and set off for the main building. At the front desk sat a young lady a couple of years his senior.

"Hi. I'm Euell Edwards. I will be attending the university next semester and I'm looking for work. I would like to teach softball and karate or self-defense. Once I send for my guitar and saxophone I would love to teach one or both of these as well as the sports I mentioned. Do you have any openings at this time?"

"There may be one coming up soon. I can give you an application that you can fill out while you are here today, or you can take it with you and return it later."

The receptionist looked through the file cabinet, found an application and handed it to Euell. Pointing to an area nearby she said, "There's a table you can use if you so desire."

The prudent thing seemed to be to fill the application out

on the spot and turn it in immediately. With that in mind, Euell sat at the table and answered all the usual, customary questions as to experience and qualifications. The problem was that he had no address or phone number to list as his own. Remembering the business card he had in his wallet, he pulled it out, copied Dr. Cunningham's phone number onto the application, and used the Christian college address as his own. When he handed the completed application back to the receptionist, she said, "Good luck", as she looked it over for completeness.

"Thanks," Euell said as he turned toward the door. When he reached his bike, he decided that the next stop would be at the Christian college and seminary.

The bike purchase had been a great idea. Euell was able to get around a lot faster than had been the case when walking was his method of transport. It was a matter of five or six minutes and he was at his next destination. He locked his bike to the stand and found the building labeled "Office of Admissions and Records."

Summer school was in session and the lines were long. Euell stood in one line for almost ten minutes when he saw an individual who appeared to be a professor walking through the lines. "Excuse, me. Do you know where Dr. Cunningham's office is located?"

"Yes, I do in fact. He's in Faculty Building One, and his office is on the second floor. But, I'm not certain that he is currently available, or even on campus. I do not believe that he is teaching a class for the summer session."

"Thank you very much," Euell said earnestly as he abandoned the line that still had not moved an inch. The Faculty Building was easy to identify. Euell climbed that stairs quickly and located Professor Cunningham's office. The door was closed. But, when Euell knocked, a voice could be heard from inside saying, "The door is unlocked. Come on in."

Euell opened the door and saw the professor hard at work at his desk, with his back to the door. Euell moved past book-lined walls and shelves that were in transition and waited for the right moment to speak.

Dr. Cunningham turned from his task and smiled brightly when he saw that it was Euell. "How are you? Here, have a seat. Have you talked with someone in Admissions and Records about your questions and concerns?"

"No. The summer session lines are long and I decided to try at another time when the lines are not likely to be as large. I'm certain that the staff would prefer that I talk with them about next semester after they have gotten this session underway."

"I'm sure you are correct in your assessment of the present situation. The fact that this is a new college with new staff and students means that there is a definite learning curve for all of us. What brings you here today?"

"My bike," Euell said jokingly.

Professor Cunningham laughed out loud. "Well, I wasn't really referring to your mode of transportation. Why did you come to see me today?"

"Sorry about my warped sense of humor. It hadn't shown itself recently."

"Humor is a good thing. I find that it helps me establish a suitable feeling tone in my classes, and it helps me through life's difficult moments. You no doubt know that Abraham Lincoln used an almost constant barrage of humor in order to make it through the Civil War, the family problems, the tension within his cabinet, and the many death threats that he received. I think his humor was one of the few things that allowed him to keep his sanity and function as Chief Executive."

"Actually, I have never heard this before."

"Well, it was not always appreciated by his advisors and those who were his most bitter critics. But, it got him through one of the toughest periods of our history and aided his deep, deep depression."

"None the less, I'll put a leash on my humor," Euell promised. "I'm here to see you about finding a good church. I was hoping that you might recommend one. And, I was wondering if you know of any part time jobs that are currently available."

"I'll address those in reverse order, if you don't mind. I haven't a clue as to any positions presently available locally, though I will keep an eye open for anything that falls into the categories we discussed previously. Well, actually anything that I think may be a good fit. As to churches, try a few around town. I don't know which denomination you prefer. But, you don't have to agree with every theological perspective of a particular church in order to worship, feel at home, and become an active part of the church family."

"I agree with you completely," Euell said. "I will find one for this Sunday. Back to the job situation. I put your phone number and the college/seminary address on my application at the Community Youth Club. I was..."

"Why not use your own address and phone number? There is little or no job advantage in an association with college personnel."

Euell explained his temporary living situation and the lack of a phone and address, and said that he had hoped that it would not be an imposition to ask for any messages to be relayed to him some way.

"Young man, I am going to have to see what I can do about getting you better, more suitable living accommodations. As to taking your call in the interim, I won't be in my office every day. I'm doing some research and writing courses. But, I can check my office messages from the home phone and contact you. Where is this place you presently call home?"

Euell gave him complete directions. Then he asked a question he had not really planned to ask. "What should I do to prepare for the Christian college and the university? What I mean is, are there certain books I should read over the summer?"

"That's the kind of question I would expect a serious student to ask. There are so many books that should be prerequisite to college. I would certainly recommend skimming academic books from various subject areas. Reviewing research skills and study skills would help considerably. Read the book of *Proverbs* more than once. Study the *Gospel of John*. Both of these books will ground you in the Judeo-Christian World and Life View. Read *Uncle Tom's Cabin* and *Les Miserables* to factor in empathy and to immerse yourself in the human condition. Watch *It's a Wonderful Life* and pay close attention to the character of George Bailey. You can come to my house to watch it, and we can discuss the movie in depth. Watch or read *A Christmas Carol*. Watch Mel Gibson's movie portrayal of Jesus' crucifixion. Of course I'm referring to *The Passion of the Christ*. Watch the inspiring story of William Wilberforce in the movie, *Amazing Grace*. If you had asked any other professor you would have gotten a different list. But, these are the ones I would recommend in order to strengthen the basics, imbed your thoughts in the Christian paradigm, illustrate practical Christianity in everyday life, remind you of the human condition, and prepare you to think critically when so much of what you know to be true is challenged."

Euell left Dr. Cunningham's office with mixed feelings. He was upbeat. But, he was worried that he could never cover all the material that had been suggested. He felt ill prepared for the college experience. And, he knew that his life had already prepared him to understand much about "the human condition".

Chapter 13

Disappointment, Stowe and Justice, A New
Start

As Euell rode away from the Christian college and seminary campus he was a bit overwhelmed with the enormity of the task at hand as well as the helpfulness of the professor. His next stop would be the university.

As he arrived at the staff parking area a professor or other
employee of the institution pointed and called out, "Student
parking for bikes-over there!" Euell wasn't sure what to make
of the command. Was the person just being helpful, or was he
being rude and demanding? Euell hoped it was the former.

Euell rode some distance before finding the bike area,
parked and locked the bike, and set out to explore the campus.
As he walked along the campus sidewalks he noticed a difference in the summer session students on the two campuses.
The overall feeling was different. Both were academic. But
there was a spiritual dimension that was lacking on the university campus. Perhaps he had made a mistake enrolling full
time here with the idea of part time on the other campus.

Euell reached into his backpack and withdrew a bag of trail

mix as he sat down on the newly mowed lawn to watch and reflect. The thought occurred to him that he may be able to use the libraries of both campuses in order to read the suggested selections.

After eating all he needed for the moment, he asked a student where the library was located and ambled off in the general direction he had been given. It was easy to find. It was a rather imposing building with the word "Library" writ large above the entrance.

The first book Euell wanted to find was Harriet Beecher Stowe's classic, *Uncle Tom's Cabin.* He located a copy and began to read parts of it word-for-word, and to skim and scan other sections. When he finished the book he had a very clear picture of the author's intent, as well as the personality and character of Uncle Tom. Euell realized that what Harriet Beecher Stowe had done for the slaves should be done for the unborn. While *Uncle Tom's Cabin* had exposed slavery for the evil institution it really was, nothing similar had been done for the right to life cause. He remembered a song called "My Name Is Justice" that someone in California had written for Johnny Cash. Though Cash apparently chose not to record the song, the singer/writer/guitarist of the song did receive some air time on a few stations. The words and melody came clearly to mind.

My name is Justice, I won't be denied

My name is Truth, and you cannot hide

I might be hidden beneath some liberal lies

But, my name is Justice and I won't be denied.

I was there at the trial when they made a mockery

They trampled and stomped constitutionality

I witnessed travesty played out by the court

As freedoms were trampled by liberal cohorts.

My name is Justice, I won't be denied

My name is Truth, and you cannot hide

I might be hidden beneath some liberal lies

But, my name is Justice and I won't be denied.

I was with Mr. Denny when hell came down

I heard the devil's thunder as he was struck down

I saw hell's fire rise all around

And I saw the evil fury as the bricks came down.

My name is Justice, I won't be denied

My name is Truth, and you cannot hide

I might be hidden beneath some liberal lies

But, my name is Justice and I won't be denied.

I heard the scream of children taken from the womb

I heard Satan laughing by the sacrificial tomb

I saw the wealthy doctors as they hurried through the room

Intent on one more baby-kill before high noon.

My name is Justice, I won't be denied

My name is Truth, and you cannot hide

I might be hidden beneath some liberal lies

But, my name is Justice and I won't be denied.

I was creator, yet I've been denied

My plan was perfect, yet Darwin decried

My love was greater that any could see

My son was murdered by man's philosophy.

My name is Justice, I won't be denied

My name is Truth, and you cannot hide

I might be hidden beneath some liberal lies

But, my name is Justice and I won't be denied.

My name is Justice, I won't be denied

My name is Truth, and you cannot hide

Alvis West

I might be hidden beneath some liberal lies

But, my name is Justice and I won't be denied.

The song lyrics pulled no punches. And, there was a little poetic license. The scream of children was of course a silent scream. Silent, that is, to human ears, but not to God's.

Euell decided to skim through as many books as time allowed in order to review for a number of subjects, and get up to speed, so-to-speak. He took the opportunity seriously as he rushed through as many subject area materials as humanly possible. In fact, he was blurry-eyed and a bit shaky when he finally exited the library at closing time.

When Euell arrived at the bike area it was obvious that someone had attempted to steal his bicycle or to pull a prank. The nuts were off the front wheel hub, and the wheel was free of the bike.

Euell picked the nuts up and put them back on the hub. He didn't have a wrench, so he tightened them as best he could by hand. He headed home to camp for the night, write letters, study Proverbs, and perhaps read the Gospel of John if he did not fall asleep from fatigue.

The next few days were very much like the first two days. There was camp to set up and tear down, the backpack to fill in the morning and empty at night, the meager meals each day, the letters written at night and mailed the next morning, the waiting for a job notification, the attempt to follow

Dr. Cunningham's advice as to reading materials, the difficulty cleaning up and doing laundry at a nearby laundromat, the on-going tour of the community, the question of the right choice of schools, the loneliness, and the nearly constant thoughts pertaining to his friends. But, one day was distinct and memorable. One morning a car pulled up near Euell's tent. Out stepped Dr. Cunningham and his friend Mr. Brighton.

"Well, Euell, are you ready for a change in venue?" asked the professor.

"Do you mean a move back home? I've thought about that many times."

Mr. Brighton spoke up. "We have something closer in mind. I have a guest house/mother-in-law unit out back that I just had remodeled. I don't want to rent it out until late August when the next semester begins. For now, it's yours rent-free. This will tide you over until you are ready to move into the university dorm."

"And, there's more good news," stated Dr. Cunningham. "The Community Youth Center called last night and left a message. You have an interview at eleven o'clock today. That is, unless you have something else to do."

"I can't believe this! I'll pack right now!"

Both men helped Euell pack and carry everything to the car. Euell knew that the bike wouldn't fit into the trunk without taking a chance of scratching the car. Therefore, he asked for directions to the house, and explained that he would ride his bike to his new home.

The Good Samaritans left behind a very happy young man. They ran two short errands on the way and barely arrived before the eager young friend.

Euell was in awe of the beautiful home and the guest house. Now he had an address to enable others to write him. Well, all but Mandy could write him. She was still in Europe and had not yet seen the many letters he had sent.

Chapter 14

Interview and the Activists

Euell rode his bike to the Community Youth Center and arrived thirty minutes early in order to observe the way the employees interacted with each other and the students. He also wanted to look over the facilities.

"I think I will really enjoy this place," he said to himself. It was a positive affirmation to bolster his confidence that he would get the job.

At the appointed time Euell was called into an office down the hallway three doors from the receptionist's desk. Seated at a long table were two people. One was a middle-aged man. The other was a woman of perhaps fifty-five years of age.

"Hello, Euell. I'm Sam Bartel and this is Edwina Sansum. We just want to confirm your responses on the application and see if the job is the right fit for you, so-to-speak."

"Fair enough," Euell replied.

Mrs. Sansum was the first to ask a question. "First of all, we noticed that you used Dr. Cunningham's office phone number and the Christian college as your address. Was there a reason for this?"

"Yes. I had no address at the time. I was living in a tent just outside of town. The landowner was kind enough to allow me to camp there until I could find a place to live. Actually, I thought I might have to wait until the fall semester at the university, at which time I will have a dorm room. But, I'm proud to say that I now have an address until the dorm is ready for occupancy. Here's the address," Euell said as he handed Mrs. Sansum a slip of paper.

Mrs. Sansum looked at the slip of paper and passed it back to Euell along with the application.

"Would you mind making the necessary changes? We would like to keep the application completely in your handwriting. I suppose Dr. Cunningham's phone number will be appropriate for now."

The paper was returned to the interviewers. They glanced at the changes and resumed the questioning.

"Is it your intent to only work for us during school breaks?" asked Mr. Bartel.

"No. I would like a part-time, year round job with the option of working full time during the summer, and perhaps other breaks as well. The main purpose for the job is to cover some expenses, chief of which is the tuition, fees, and books at the Christian college and seminary where I plan to attend part time. At the university I will be full time on a full scholarship."

Mrs. Sansum looked rather serious as she asked, "Mr.

Edwards, how will you ever be able to keep up with your studies in two colleges and hold down a job? That's a very full schedule."

"And attend church," Euell added. Then he gave them a brief history of the many activities he had been involved in while in junior high school and high school, as well as the fact that he had maintained grades sufficient to obtain a full scholarship. "I have always taken on many responsibilities. Each one, academic or not, receives my full attention and effort."

The two administrators looked at each other with a combination of expressions that revealed surprise, satisfaction, and concern.

"You are qualified to teach karate, self defense, softball, saxophone, and guitar. Is this correct?" asked Mr. Bartel.

"That is correct. I can also perform music as a solo artist or with a band if there is ever a function for which this is needed. I will immediately send for my karate ghee, saxophone, and guitar as soon as I know that I have the job."

Mrs. Sansum said, "We will need documentation as to your black belt certification, as well as letters of recommendation from your hardware store manager."

"No problem. I will ask my mother to mail the actual certificate along with the other things I mentioned."

Mrs. Sansum asked politely, "Will you excuse us for a few minutes? You can wait by the receptionist's desk and we will call for you as soon as we have made a decision."

Euell felt good about the interview. He felt that he had given honest, complete answers to each of the questions that had come his way. So he sat quietly contemplating how life at the youth club would be. All in all it should be a good experience and additional income. But, as time passed Euell had not been called back into the room. He began to question whether or not he had gotten the job, and then he began to panic. Why hadn't he applied for other jobs instead of spending his time doing other things, useful as they may have been at the time?

The interviewee stood for awhile, sat for awhile, walked around the room, then looked at the trophy case and pictures of present and past students and instructors. Next, he stood looking out the window. What could possibly be taking so much time? Did they doubt his word? Did the small smudge he had just discovered on his shirt discourage a positive decision? Was it customary to take this long to make a decision? Did he really have cause to worry? Where would he find another job? Would it be as interesting as this one seemed? Did the administrators think that he was a deadbeat loser because he had been living in a tent? Why hadn't he suggested demonstrating his karate and self defense skills? Perhaps he should have already had his ghee, guitar, and saxophone sent in anticipation of this interview.

Finally, after what seemed an eternity, Mr. Bartel opened the door and invited Euell to return to the interview room.

Once Euell was seated, the two administrators looked at each other briefly and Mr. Bartel nodded for Mrs. Sansum to continue where they had left off previously.

She said, "I am very sorry that..."

Euell interrupted her unintentionally by stating, "I desperately need this job. I am dependable, loyal, and qualified. Please..." Euell stopped talking because Mrs. Sansum was holding her hand up like it was a stop sign.

"I was going to say, I am very sorry that we took so long and that we kept you waiting. We would like to see a demonstration of some kind. But, relax. We both agree that you have the job. I guess this is really just a formality so that we can say that we actually saw you exhibit some of your talent."

Euell was visibly relieved and gladly demonstrated some of the techniques of karate and self defense.

Mr. Barton asked, "Can you come in full time for the next two weeks? This is a paid training seminar that covers all aspects of orientation, rules and regulations, first aid, CPR, exercise theories, scheduling, room use, teaching styles, and a little practical experience in virtually every job we offer on this campus."

"Yes!" Euell replied immediately.

"Then we will see you Monday at 8:00 A.M. Of course there will be others taking the classes with you," stated Mr. Bartel.

Euell could barely contain his enthusiasm. He was jubilant to say the least. Two weeks of full time work would help his economic condition tremendously. It would boost his confidence as well. Now he really had something to write home about.

On his way home to his new residence, Euell noticed a

rather large gathering in an otherwise empty lot. His curiosity caused him to stop and listen.

The speaker was saying, "The legislative and judicial branches of the United States government have failed the American people by ignoring the clear intent of the United States Constitution, especially as pertaining to the Bill of Rights; favoring views by anti-American special interests groups such as the American Civil Liberties Union and Americans United for Separation of Church and State; allowing judicial tyranny through legislation from the bench; attempting to make Christians second class citizens; disallowing rights for the unborn as the ultimate form of presumption; using taxpayer money to pay for ungodly, uncivilized, inhumane, Third Reich experimentation on aborted babies; allowing America to become a culture of child molestation; allowing the airwaves to become open sewers; attempting to limit Christian activism by forcing Christian groups to register as lobbyists; deciding the Kello v. London case in favor of the extension of government rights relative to eminent domain and the subsequent diminishing of the right to private ownership of land; promoting socialistic ideology, secular humanism, and the theory of evolution over creationism or intelligent design; the forced removal of crosses and other symbols of our faith and heritage from public places as an open door for their eventual removal from non-public places. The excuse is that someone, somewhere has been offended by the Christian symbols. I am offended by their anti-Christian bigotry. But, I have not sued any of the anti-religionists. Not yet, anyway."

At this point in his speech, a small group of radical liberals started chanting and yelling so loudly that the speaker could not be heard. Euell kept a safe distance as the angry liberal left ranted, raved, and used foul language in an all-out attempt to dissuade the speaker from going any further. There were only a few police officers on the scene. But, suddenly, from seemingly all directions, police cars arrived and uniformed officers sprang from their cars armed with riot gear. Some of the officers set up a protective barrier around the peaceful group that had been listening to the speaker on the small, impromptu stage. Other officers directed traffic. A third group of officers began the process of arresting the agitators.

Meanwhile the crowd waited patiently for the resumption of the speech.

Chapter 15

Activism

Freedom of speech won the day. The speaker calmly returned to the microphone and continued the pro-conservative, pro-Christian speech.

"The answer to the long list of usurpation is not another American Revolution. This would invariably end in anarchy. The answer may be partially found in a new political party. The Democratic Party has been the main culprit when it comes to pushing ideology from the liberal extreme and when it comes to playing Robin Hood with the taxpayers' hard earned money. But, the Republican Party has been so interested in seeking favor from the Democratic centrists and the voters that it has been reluctant to take a strong stand on the moral and ethical issues for fear of losing an election or causing factionalism. I believe that politicians are too concerned with the next election. True statesmen and stateswomen are more concerned with the next generation. I wish we had more statesmen and stateswomen with the moral and ethical backbone to stand up for the things that made America the great nation it was until anti-Christian factions began their efforts to dismantle America and re-write the history books so that history appeared to support their personal ideologies.

Home teaching may be another partial answer. Political correctness has destroyed the public school system. So has the 'dumbing down' of the curriculum and the secularization of our school systems. In the colonial period the Bible was the textbook, morality and ethics were taught in the schools. In the seventeenth and eighteenth centuries Harvard, William and Mary, Yale, Princeton, Columbia, Brown, Rutgers, and Dartmouth were birthed by Christians. Christian charity eventually developed to the point that various denominations were tolerated. So were Judaism and atheism. Over the course of American history a pluralistic society developed. We Christians allowed non-believers into our boat. Now they want to kick us out of the boat! But, whatever happens to the religious liberty of Christians will eventually happen to the Jews, Muslims, and all others with religiously based world and life views.

Only recently have I entertained the thought of leaving America as a result of the items previously mentioned. I have had my fill of the imposition of socialistic ideologies, secular humanism, militant atheism, anti-Christian bigotry, the lack of decency, the lack of respect, and the fact that the theory of evolution and its implications via Social Darwinism are taught as gospel truth. I am sickened by the proliferation of drugs, gangs, violence, reckless driving, crime, volitional idiocy, and by the very idea that Hillary Clinton could become the next president of the United States of America. Most troubling of all is the fact that a very large percentage of our elected officials, and those appointed to the courts, have forgotten that this is a government of the people, by the people, and for the people. May God enlighten our leaders and our citizens before it is too late."

The crowd gave a thunderous roar of applause that continued for some time. Finally, another speaker walked onto the stage and waited for the crowd to finish showing its enthusiasm for the ideologies just expressed. When the applause died down, the speaker said, "Did you notice that the ACLU types wanted to silence us? Keep in mind that in Skokie, Illinois, in the year of our Lord, 1977, the ACLU was the very group that defended the right of the KKK and neo-Nazis to march in the Fourth of July parade. Anti-Semitic, anti-Catholic, and anti-Black speech is deemed worthy of protection by the ACLU. Yet, our freedom of expression relative to traditional values, and our Christian heritage are offensive and an outrage that they must stop! What a distortion of freedom of expression! It seems that an extreme liberal can stand and tell you with a straight face that he has the real meaning behind the Bill of Rights. According to many of these fine folks, the founders did not really mean what they said, scholars for the last two hundred years did not really understand what the founders meant, and conservatives today do not understand a thing about the original intent of such things as the first amendment. Funny, isn't it? I, and many other scholars, have read the United

States Constitution, the Federalist Papers, the Anti-Federalist Papers, and scores of related documents many times over. Yet, an extreme liberal will tell us we have a fundamental misunderstanding of the intent and meaning. In other words, they tell us that black is white and white is black, and call us stupid because we do not believe them! I'm sorry, this was not what I planned to say today. But, the rude attempt to silence us today underscores the reason we are here! Now, to the speech I prepared."

The crowd exploded in a massive show of enthusiasm for the truths the speaker had so eloquently, bravely, and forcefully spoken.

"We have allowed our collective political voices to atrophy by pusillanimously allowing the ACLU and other anti-Christian and anti-American organizations to bully us into submission. We have stood by as they have preached an unhealthy toleration for trashy entertainment, and have shown a total disdain for traditional American values and traditions. We have stood silently as they have taken the tax exempt status from a church that allowed a politically conservative speech, and as anti-traditionalists misused the right of eminent domain for the purpose of obtaining church property for the construction of a retail store. We have muted our voices as they defended hate-filled speeches by the Ku Klux Klan and the Neo-Nazis. We have cowered down as they effectually removed voluntary prayer from our public schools, and as they have found legal ways to muzzle those who believe in the sanctity of life. We have remained silent as they have challenged the five foundational rights enumerated in the first amendment to the United States Constitution. We have put our careers and personal expediency ahead of the common good and the blessings of liberty for future generations. We have watched as they have attempted to remove 'In God We Trust' from our currency. Now they want to deny our progeny the right and responsibility of saying the Pledge of Allegiance. They ignore the historic record that clearly places the first meeting of the House of Burgesses in a church in Jamestown, Virginia; the Christian founding of almost all of our first colleges; the fact that Benjamin Franklin suggested that each session of the Constitutional Convention begin with prayer for guidance from God; Jefferson's letter to the Danbury Baptists that assured them that there would be no governmental preference given to a particular denomination like there had been with the taxpayer supported Anglican Church under British rule, and Jefferson's insistence on filling government buildings in Washington, D.C. with Christian congregations holding Sunday services. We must put our time, effort, and resources toward the common good in the ongoing struggle to keep our traditional, philosophically sound, American values alive in the marketplace of ideologies!"

After much applause, the final speaker was announced and stepped to the microphone on center stage.

"What I have to offer you today is a comparison of our death cult society and that of the pagans from antiquity. Notice the striking similarities. Pagan societies exposed their unwanted babies to the elements or threw them into the Tiber River. We 'Civilized' people have them aborted and thrown away. Pagans sacrificed their children for the greater good of the people. We are presently considering stem cell research that takes a life to save, or enrich, another life. Pagans crucified Christians or threw them into the arena for mortal combat. Today, the American Civil Liberties Union continues this tradition in as far as the law of our land currently allows. Thus far the crucifixion and combat has been verbal, political and legal. Pagans had gladiatorial games. We have the modern equivalent in our entertainment industry. Of course ours is vicarious. But, some violent criminals have admitted that a particular violent movie influenced their criminal behavior. From my vantage ground, I would say that our postmodern era is nothing more than repackaged paganism. May God forgive us our blind subservience to the evil forces that now pervade our culture. And, may we vow to fight for the heart and soul of America with the strength only God can supply."

Applause followed.

Euell agreed with the principal points the speakers had made. Yet, he had a few questions for which he would have to eventually find answers. But, for now he needed to prepare for his new job and the college-readiness readings that had been suggested to him by Dr. Cunningham. The sequence was set. It would be livelihood, education, and the application of all knowledge to the glory and honor of God.

Chapter 16

Home and Enlightenment

Euell included his new, temporary address in his letters home. All those to whom he frequently wrote already possessed his future university mailing address and the college phone number in case of an emergency.

The guest-house was so much more convenient and comfortable than living in a tent. It was closer to the college and the main part of town. It was air conditioned for summer and heated for winter. The bed was so much more comfortable than the sleeping bag could ever be. The shower was almost heaven compared to the arduous daily task of bathing with wet-nap towellettes. The house didn't have to be folded up and put away, then taken out and reassembled each day. Clothing and other items did not have to be packed and unpacked each day. Clothing was easy to clean thanks to a small washer and dryer in the unit. There was room for the bike, tent, and miscellaneous items in the single car garage. It was for these things and more that Euell gave thanks to God, and to the gracious Good Samaritan that God had placed in his path. It was somewhat a matter of serendipity. And, it wasn't due to Euell's perfectly saint-like behavior. He knew that he wasn't perfect. He had never claimed to be. But, he was working on it a little each day.

Euell had given a great deal of thought to the activistic speeches he had heard the day before. Initially he had agreed with most of the discourse, though some of it seemed vehement and excessive at first. But, as he considered the speeches in light of the nation's overall condition he began to realize that he could agree with virtually everything that had been said. Our country was truly at war for the heart, mind, and soul of the people.

Bill Brighton happened to be carrying out his garbage as Euell stepped out of his little abode. "Can I help you with the garbage?" he offered sincerely.

"No thanks, Euell. I've got it this time."

After Mr. Brighton emptied his trash into the large cans he walked over to Euell. "How did the job interview go yesterday?"

"It went very well. I was hired, and I begin Monday. For the first two weeks I will be going through full time training and then I will work part time this summer and through the first semester. I may get to work full time through some or all of the school breaks, but not this summer. I have sent for my karate ghee, softball mitt, guitar, and saxophone. Oh, yeah. And, my black belt certification as well. I will be teaching karate, self defense, softball, guitar, and saxophone. This will provide the money for the Christian college classes. I can't wait!"

"How are your accommodations? Are you comfortable and settled in yet?"

"Absolutely. I couldn't wish for any more. In fact, I would like to reimburse you or work off my debt in some way."

"You don't have to do a thing. I'm glad I could help you out. Dr. Cunningham and I noticed immediately that you are not of the spoiled rich kid type, and that you have drive and purpose. You are determined to succeed and seem to be a genuinely nice person who happens to need a little assistance at this time."

"Well, it is true that I have to work hard for everything I have. But, that's a good thing. I don't take things for granted, and I see the world differently than most of those from my generation. I believe that all the world owes me is an equal opportunity-a fighting chance-nothing more, nothing less."

Euell's comments reaffirmed Mr. Brighton's confidence in him and made him proud that he had been at the right place at the right time to have met him.

Euell changed the topic of conversation somewhat. "I was downtown when some rather interesting things were happening. There were some conservative speakers who spoke about the direction our nation is taking, and the role of Christians in our society. An angry liberal mob tried to create a disturbance. But, it was quickly controlled. What do you know about the speakers? Were they local people?"

"I know one of the speakers. He is a good man, a good citizen, and a good Christian. He's a zealot of sorts. And, he is convinced that the government has turned against us as many of the leaders move closer and closer to some form of socialism. He writes many letters to his representatives. They rarely respond. When they do respond it is generally a form letter that has nothing to do with his concerns and may even list things for which he has never written. The likelihood of the elected officials having actually read his letters is not great. An aid most likely skims some of the mail and decides which pieces to pass on to the elected official. Many of the letters are probably trashed without having been read. The focus of his concerns usually ties to the American Civil Liberties Union-the ACLU-and its attempt to dismantle American and rebuild it in its own ugly image. Of course there are other hate groups out there. But, in his estimation, and mine as well, this group is the most dangerous. But, I really don't believe that the ACLU lawyers are really stupid enough to actually believe half of what they say. They are just trying to divide and conquer an already 'factionalized' nation. They function much as the early socialist party in America. They believe that the best way to destroy a nation is from within. With this in mind, they don't have to create a problem, they just exacerbate it. For example, they didn't create teenage rebellion, sexually transmitted diseases, abortion, homosexual activism, socialism, racism, teen pregnancy, or hatred of Christ and Christianity. They use divisiveness, twisted logic, and outright misinformation in order to spin their web of deceit."

"Why isn't something done to stop them?" asked Euell with fire in his voice.

"Some people have tried and some continue to try. But the ACLU is supported by many very wealthy liberals. The abortion industry certainly supports that most un-American of institutions. I was on the campus of UCLA not long ago and picked up a copy of their newspaper called the 'Daily Bruin'. I had some time to kill before an appointment, so I read the paper in its entirety. There were some good articles. Then I ran across something in the classified section. Students were offered a job helping defend the Bill of Rights and restore constitutional protections. The pay was five to eight thousand dollars for the summer job. The employer was Grassroots Campaigns Inc. on behalf of the ACLU! I could not believe my eyes. Letting them safeguard our Bill of Rights is tantamount to letting Adolf Hitler watch over the healthcare of the Jews."

"I need to learn more about some of these groups and the issues they oppose. Are there any sources you would recommend?"

"There are a few that I have found to be very helpful relative to the changing intellectual climate in America. For example, *How Then Should We Live? The Rise and Decline of Western Thought,* by Francis A. Shaeffer, *Indefensible: Ten Ways the ACLU is Destroying America,* by Sam Kastensmidt, *The Marketing of Evil,* by David Kupelian, *A Nation Without a Conscience,* by Tim and Beverly Lahaye, *Listen, America,* by Jerry Falwell, *Keeping Christ in Christmas,* by David C. Gibbs,

Jr. and David C. Gibbs III, *America: To Pray or Not to Pray,* by David Barton, *Original Intent: The Courts, the Constitution, and Religion* by David Barton, *The Christian, the Court and the Constitution: Your Rights as a Christian Citizen,* by Jay Alan Sekulow, *Gag Order: How an Unjust Law is Being Used to Silence Pastors,* by Gary Cass, *One Nation Under God,* by Dr. David C. Gibbs, Jr. with Jerry Newcombe, *America: A Call to Greatness,* by John W. Chalfant, *What's Wrong With Same Sex Marriages?* by Dr. D. James Kennedy and Jerry Newcombe. Of course there are many other titles that every American should read. I will write a list of the ones I mentioned and drop it into your door's mail slot."

"I don't know how soon I will be able to read any of the sources you mentioned. My reading list is long and I haven't even started college yet!"

"Yes, I know the feeling well. It is overwhelming. I try to read the books that seem to be of greatest significance. My list continues to grow and grow. In your case, most of the books will likely have to be read at semester break or even after you finish college and graduate school. Of course you could join a literary society where each individual learns one book well and shares it with the other members, or learn to skim, scan, and speed read to obtain the main points. Our political activism is badly needed at this very moment."

Euell went home and reflected on what he had heard from the activists and Mr. Brighton. He knew that he had to become part of the solution. Yet, there was much to read, absorb, understand, and apply. This would mean immersion in many sources. But, before he allowed himself to become completely overwhelmed, he recalled one of his favorite high school teachers telling the class that he had to wait until after college to find the time to attack the reading list he had written for himself as he discovered so many books, magazines, and scholarly journals that were worthy of his time, attention, and opportunity costs.

Chapter 17

Sensei Edwards and Injured Pride

Euell was excited that his two-week training at the Community Youth Center was over and that he finally had a paycheck in his hand. All of the items he had requested from home were now in his possession and ready to be put to use on the job. He was ready to rock 'n' roll, as they say.

On the first night of karate class Euell thought he would wow the new practitioners with his knowledge, speed, power, and overall techniques. He began by giving a brief history of karate and several other martial arts, comparing and contrasting as he went along, but never criticizing any of the other systems. He selected various students for different technique demonstrations. The students were target dummies, minus the actual contact. He threw every kind of punch, strike, block and kick that he knew. Then he demonstrated takedowns and holds. Next came a rapid-fire demonstration of self-defense. But, the capstone of his introduction to karate was a jump kick or flying side-kick into the side of a kicking bag situated between two rows of new students. He explained how much practice was required for this kind of technique and said jokingly, "Now, don't try this one at home. Well, not yet anyway."

As Euell quickly walked to the starting position he said, "Pay particular attention as to where the jump starts, the point at which my left leg thrusts forward, and the specific human target area I would have struck with my left heel. Notice this in relation to an attack on a person of roughly my height."

Euell ran as fast as he could until he reached his chosen launching point. Just as he started his launch, and prepared for the alignment maneuver, he slipped and fell. His body was uncontrollably heading in the direction of the bag. He slid under and past his intended target. When he stood up on shaky legs, he noticed that most of the students were trying to stifle their laughter.

Euell had embarrassment written all over his face and pain emanating from his gluteus maximus. One of the students broke the silence with his insight. "I think I can answer your questions about where each part of your demonstration began. Your jump began where the sand was on the floor. As you fell, your legs kind of flopped back and forth from side to side. And, your kick would have landed on the top of your attacker's foot." Everyone cracked up. So did Euell.

"Well, I told you not to try this at home. Now you know why."

The rest of the session was taken with stretching, exercising, learning stances, and learning how to make an airtight fist.

Euell knew that his fall earlier in the evening had make him look foolish and anything but graceful. But, at the end of the session he felt good about the class. Each of the students would have their falls and embarrassing moments just as he had. Hopefully, not as hard as he had fallen, or with as many close proximity witnesses. But, it isn't *that* you fall that counts. It's how you get back up. That's a lesson that applies to all aspects of life, not just karate.

When Euell got home he decided to soak in a tub of Epson Salt and listen to the radio. He dialed in station after station until he ran across an oldies station that made him think of his uncle who had played in a nineteen fifties and early nineteen sixties rock 'n' roll band. His uncle's favorites were Buddy Holly and the Crickets, Chuck Berry, Ricky Nelson, Elvis Presley, Eddie Cochran, Connie Francis, Fats Domino, Duane Eddy, Johnny and the Hurricanes, Little Richard, The Coasters, The Platters, The Drifters, Roy Orbison, Carl Perkins, The Olympics, Jan and Arnie (later to be Jan and Dean), The Beach Boys, and The Ventures. There were others, but Euell couldn't remember their names at the moment.

The long bath and the music made him relax to the point that he thought it was time to get some work done. He dried off and dressed comfortably. The first job was to read letters. He read Frank's letter first and was surprised to learn that Frank had opened a real estate business that was already doing well. He still taught karate classes and self defense with Sensei Brown. Next was a letter from John. This contained even better news. It seems that John's father had thought about Euell's request that the family continue trying to find a church in which they were comfortable. They had found such a church and the whole family had accepted Jesus as their personal Lord and Savior. They had been born again as the Bible describes it in the third chapter of the Gospel of John.

There was no letter from Euell's mother. This was indeed no surprise. It had been very difficult to get her to send the items he needed for his job, even though Euell had sent a ca-shiers check that more than covered the shipping costs.

The next chore was to write his nightly letters. In the letter to John he said, "If Mandy happens to contact you, tell her that I need to speak with her ASAP." Then Euell realized that he would not have a phone until he moved to the university dorm. So he gave John the number for Mr. Brighton's residence, real-izing all the while that he should have asked permission prior to giving it to anyone.

Karate practice was next. Sore or not, Euell put in a good twenty minutes doing katas in the single car garage until he reached his limit. He now realized that riding a bicycle, sit-ting for any length of time, or most any kind of physical ex-ercise would be difficult at best until some of the pain and discomfort from the fall had dissipated. For this particular evening he could only go through the motions slowly as he kind of practiced throwing, catching and batting without ac-tually using a ball or a bat. When he went back into his house he turned the radio on and listened while he tuned his guitar. For quite some time he played guitar along with the songs on the radio, then switched to saxophone and did the same thing.

As Euell put everything away, he noticed a note on the floor near the front door. It was the list of suggested books that Mr. Brighton had mentioned previously. He read through the list in order to become familiar with the titles and authors. If he did this regularly for a while, he wouldn't have to keep the list for anything more than a souvenir.

Euell placed his outgoing letters into the postal pickup box attached to the front of his temporary abode before he set out for a short walk to help take away some of the inevitable stiffness and soreness. He almost laughed out loud when he thought of how silly the fall must have appeared. If he had been a spectator instead of the perpetrator/victim, he would have likely laughed at the sight. No one should take himself too seriously.

As Euell walked and thought, he heard a dog barking from a nearby yard. This was enough to get him thinking about the future. Wouldn't it be nice to be married, have a dog and a cat, finish college and graduate school, and really make a difference in the lives of his friends, relatives, associates, and the world at large? It would be such a waste of God-given life not to do all that he could to help make the world a better place. Tomorrow held so many possibilities.

Euell walked back to the little house so that he could read his Bible and pray. Both activities gave him strength, purpose, and resolve. They also brought him mind to mind and heart to heart with his creator and closest friend.

Chapter 18

Pastor Wilson versus Mere Theories

Riding a bike proved to be just as pain provoking as Euell had thought it would be. Actually it was even more uncomfortable than he had expected. But, he had to be able to get from place to place very quickly. Walking would not be fast enough.

Euell's first stop was at the church he had joined and attended regularly. He noticed that the pastor looked like he was doing several jobs at once. Perhaps this was not the time to ask some rather detailed questions.

"Pastor Wilson, are you too busy to talk for a few minutes?"

"No, not at all, son. Come on in and have a seat if you like. I will pile these papers in separate stacks and be right with you."

Euell sat down outside the pastor's office and picked up a copy of *Christianity Today*. In the Culture Comment section was an article by Darrel Bock, research professor of New Testament studies at Dallas Theological Seminary. The title of the article caught Euell's eye. It was entitled, "The Good

News of Da Vinci." It was, of course, about the popular book written by Dan Brown. Euell had heard that the book was a good read, though horribly flawed theologically and in matters directly related to the historicity of some of the organizations portrayed as non-fictional.

Euell had read other material that had challenged Dan Brown's assertions. These included a booklet RBC Ministries had published challenging some aspects of the novel. Also challenging some truth claims embedded in the book were *The Da Vinci Deception*, by Edwin W. Lutzer, and *The Da Vinci Myth Versus the Gospel Truth*, by Dr. D. James Kennedy and Jerry Newcombe.

Each one of the sources was valuable in getting at the truth. Dr. Bock's approach was that of using the controversy to tell the true story of Jesus to those curious enough to ask questions and discuss something that was cerebral, significant, and potentially life changing.

Euell had almost finished reading the article when Pastor Wilson announced, "I've cleaned up all I can for now. Come on in."

The pastor motioned to a chair across from his desk and Euell sat down ready to discuss some issues that were on his mind.

"How can I help you, Son?"

"I was on the university campus and overheard a group of students discussing Jesus' resurrection. One of the students seemed to accept the resurrection as possible. The others did not. In fact, one of them started challenging the very possibility of miracles, especially of a miraculous resurrection, by using a number of counter theories that I had never heard of before. Are you familiar with the theories to which he was referring?"

"Oh, yes indeed. Theories like these, and other anti-Christian propaganda, appear all the time. But, they generally appear around Easter. Some people can not stand the fact that there are people who have found that faith and truth intersect at the cross of Jesus."

"How credible are these challenges to the faith?"

"I'll tell you the various arguments against the resurrection of Christ as messiah in general, as well as the Christian defense of the faith called apologetics, and let you decide who has the strongest argument to support their case.

First was the Jewish response to the resurrection. It said that the disciples had stolen Jesus' body. That same story has been resurrected/revived and revised by Deists. But, for the story to be true we have to believe that the formerly frightened disciples would have suddenly gained their courage, been able to slip past trained Roman soldiers, moved a two ton rock up an incline without making any noise, taken other risks by hanging around long enough to remove Jesus' grave clothing, folded them neatly, and placed them in a conspicuous place. The story raises the question of sleeping guards being able to identify the thieves and yet not being willing to stop them, and the fact that there was a severe punishment or even death for dereliction of duty. And, what about the written accounts of the disciples as sincere, good, and honest individuals? Besides, the distraught disciples were not psychologically prepared for a conspiracy. What the story does tell us with a great degree of certainty is that Jesus was indeed buried in a tomb.

Another theory has robbers stealing Jesus' body. Why would they steal the body and leave the clothing? The material was of fine new linen that would have some monetary value. Of what value was a corpse? There were risks involved. What would have happened if the Roman soldiers had caught the thieves? Besides, carrying a nude body around would likely draw some unwanted attention.

Some skeptics have said that the Jewish and Roman authorities stole Christ's body or moved it to a more secure location. This is a very week argument indeed. If the authorities had in fact taken the body for any reason, they would have surely displayed it in public once the stories of the resurrection and appearances became known. Producing the body would have ended the speculation and stopped the spread of the new movement."

"A really strange theory has the more emotional disciples hallucinating Jesus' appearances as a result of recalling his stories and teachings, and the weather conditions of the clear Galilean air. But, hallucinations are a private experience. Appearing to five hundred people at one time is hardly private. Besides, there were varying degrees of commitment to Christ and various levels of understanding as to his relationship to the father. Some 'scholars' have even postulated 'telegrams from heaven'. Again, all the authorities- if they had the body and wanted to stop the spread of a falsehood-had to do was display the body of Jesus the Christ.

The swoon theory has Jesus reviving from the coolness of the tomb and trading his grave garb for gardeners' clothing. This would mean that Jesus had been able to overcome the injuries and shock from the brutal beating and crucifixion; survive three days without medical care, food and water; and deal with the approximately eighty pounds of spices that were applied to his dressings after his death. He would then be required to move the two-ton rock up an incline, overpower the trained guards, and walk several miles to Emmaus. Imagine a person whose flesh is torn away from his back and legs and his bones are exposed. He has holes in his wrists and feet, as well as a gaping hole in his side. His head shows the marks of the crown of thorns and his beard has been pulled out. This individual would have to walk the distance, and then inspire the disciples to carry out the Great Commission. What incentive would his followers have? They had nothing to gain if their master had only revived and managed to hobble over to them. This would not have been the conquering messiah Jesus clearly claimed to be. Another reason for not accepting this preposterous theory is that the Roman soldiers knew from much brutal experience when a man was dead. The reason they did not have to break Jesus' legs, and thus hasten death by asphyxiation, was that they corroborated their belief that Jesus was dead by thrusting a spear into his side, thus piercing the pericardium. The separate flow of blood and water proved that Jesus was no longer physically alive. Even though the theory is full of holes, it gets resurrected in various forms from time to time.

One of the weirdest, most off the wall theories is that Jesus had an identical twin brother that was taken from Mary at birth, reappeared after the crucifixion, and pretended to be Jesus to fool his followers. But, where is the evidence for this story? Would Mary not recognize that this was not Jesus? Where was this mysterious twin during Jesus' life on earth? How did he hear about the crucifixion of his brother? What did he have to gain by deceiving the disciples?

There are other theories. These include the wrong tomb theories, the merely spiritual resurrection theory, and the unknown tomb theory. All of them fail under close scrutiny. Atheists, agnostics, skeptics, materialists, secular humanists, anti-religionists, rationalists, those who hold views common to Hinduism, Buddhism, Islam, Judaism, Confucianism and other Chinese philosophies, Satanism, Neo-Paganism, and liberal Christian theologians have attacked the Biblical story of the Resurrection. Some of them have raised questions based on supposed biblical contradictions. But, most of these can be easily explained via exegetical analysis. Some have questioned the veracity of the story based on misunderstandings about secular sources as they appear to disagree with the biblical record. The list goes on and on. Finally, one has to realize that all truth is narrow, and that omniscience is not within the purview of mere mortals.

I hope that I have given you enough information so that you can make some informed decisions. Keep your eyes open to what you see all around you. Do some research on the topic when you can make the time."

Euell seemed almost overwhelmed. "I didn't realize that there were so many theories opposing the resurrection. I suppose that anyone with an ax to grind will find a way, regardless of how weak it is, to discredit what he does not understand and cannot therefore accept. But, most of the theories you mentioned would have required major miracles to have occurred in order for them to have been plausible."

"Precisely," Pastor Wilson said emphatically. "And you will find that David Hume and other like-minded individuals denied, a priori, the very possibility of a genuine miracle. Of course this smacks of man's arrogance, and man's pretensions of omniscience. It kind of reminds you of the Garden of Eden experience between those made in God's image and the deceiver."

Chapter 19

Painful Reminiscing

Euell sat outside his guest-house pondering the recent events of his life and their significance. He knew that everything works for the good of those who love God and are the called according to his purpose. His life experiences, the biblical teaching on this issue, and something akin to intuition told him that the recent events would also work to his good. His life's hard knocks had made him tough and independent while at the same time making him tender and understanding toward others. These attributes were building blocks for success.

Euell had met people who had made a vast difference in his life. Some of them still were making a difference. One day it would be his turn to aid and to influence others. To some degree he was already engaged in this charitable enterprise. He influenced his students at the Community Youth Center. This was the case in all the classes he taught in karate, self-defense, softball, saxophone, and guitar. Acutely aware of this fact, he tried to squeeze in things of eternal significance. But, he had to be very careful because of the students, parents and staff members that may be anti-Christian or resent any reference to spiritual things.

One thing that Euell wanted to understand was himself. He wanted to know why he held certain opinions and why he did certain things. Yet, he knew that introspection could not be completely objective.

The longer Euell sat and pondered, the more deeply he fell into introspection. He thought back on his earliest memories. There was a man who used to come around once in a while. But, Euell's mental picture of the man was blurry at best. He had asked his mother about the man on numerous occasions. Each time she had pretended having no knowledge of him at all. He also seemed to remember his mother being gone and having left him alone more than once. There were numerous occasions of his mother coming home barely able to walk, and vomiting all over the furniture and flooring. The mess would usually be cleaned up by midmorning the next day.

When Euell was taken to kindergarten on the first day he was so frightened that he messed his pants. His mother brought him one of the only other pairs of shorts and pants that he owned. And, she gave him a severe scolding and admonition. She made it crystal clear that she had no intention of ever coming back to mollycoddle him. Regardless of the tough start, Euell made it through kindergarten without much difficulty. His teacher seemed to like him. This was the beginning of his interest in school and learning in general. In fact, it gave him a reason to exist.

First grade was all right. The only thing that stood out in his mind was the time that he had become ill at school and his mother had to come and pick him up. She was not very happy about the intrusion into her time.

In second grade Euell had two friends whom he would never forget. One was Judy, and the other was Robert. They played tag and raced each other almost every recess. Sometimes they played tetherball. The year was going so well that he thought it would be great to stay in second grade forever. But, both of his friends moved before the end of the school year, leaving Euell very much alone.

Fourth grade was a turning point for Euell. He started to notice that people had begun to treat him differently. And, it didn't take too long to discover the reason. One day he went into the boy's rest room at recess. A boy he barely knew came in, looked at Euell, checked to see that no one else was watching, and punched him in the solar plexis so hard that he lost all his breath and fell to his knees. The boy fired a parting shot, "That's for wearing dorky looking clothes."

As the bully left, two other boys came into the rest room. By this time Euell was on his feet and bent over slightly while holding his stomach area with his right hand. If Euell had expected sympathy he was certainly wrong. One of the boys asked, "What's the matter with you?" When there was no answer he continued, "Can't you talk?"

The two boys took care of the business that had prompted them to enter the rest room in the first place, and the big-mouthed boy decided to get in one more dig. "Don't your mommy even know how to dress you?" The boys laughed in a phony kind of way as they exited the room. And, Euell was not about to stop them to correct the one boy's grammar.

Euell tried to straighten his clothing and get back to class as quickly as he possibly could. Nonetheless, he arrived late. The teacher had asked him why he was late and he had told the teacher that he had been sick at his stomach. That brought laughter from the class. Someone must have told some of them what had happened.

The restroom incident was so traumatizing and humiliating that Euell had tried everything he could to avoid using the school facilities. That meant holding out for a restroom until he could go home at the end of the school day. Obviously, this could not last for long. One day Euell was desperate for a rest room. There was no way he could wait until he got home. He ran in quickly, took care of business, washed his hands, and started out the door. Suddenly the bully pushed the door open wide and stepped in. Euell's heart sank as the boy asked, "What are you doing in here, wimp?"

Euell did not know what to say, so he said nothing.

"Hey, Dork! I'm talking to you!" That having been said, he hit Euell in the solar plexis, then headed for the door. But, his forward progress was impeded by the intrusion of a teacher who had heard a commotion coming from the rest room and had decided to investigate the matter.

"Wait just a minute, young man!" commanded the teacher as he reached for the bully's arm. Looking at the pain in Euell's eyes and back at the bully, the teacher demanded, "What have you done to this boy?"

"Nothing. He's just sick, that's all."

Euell managed to tell the teacher, in a halting manner, exactly what had transpired this day and on a previous day.

Both students were taken to the principal's office. This was the first time for Euell and he was obviously frightened. But, the principal tried to calm him down by putting his hand on Euell's shoulder momentarily while he sternly told the bully to sit down.

Turning his full attention on the bully, the principal asked, "Why are you picking on this young man? Don't give me some crazy story. You and I have talked about this kind of behavior more that once."

It appeared that the boy was not going to offer an explanation to the principal. So the principal moved closer to the boy and leaned close to his face. "We are still waiting for an answer!"

"Because I don't like the way he looks and his clothes."

"Well, I guess that's as good as any other excuse you have used in the past." Turning to Euell he said, "My secretary will give you an excused late pass for class. I'm sorry this happened. But, I do *not* believe it will happen again."

That night would always be in Euell's memory. His uncle came to his house with some packages. "Euell, I've been planning to do this for some time. There are some new shirts, pants, and pairs of sox in the bags. There is also a pair of shoes. I looked in your closet a few days ago and got the sizes. And, if something doesn't fit, your mother can exchange it at the store. There's a receipt in the bag. And, based on what I have heard, you are going to have to learn to take up for yourself. Maybe I should enroll you in a boxing club or in judo or something."

Euell's uncle stayed and talked with him for a little over an hour. He had done that many times before. And, Euell understood why. But, Euell never forgot that evening, and he never would. His uncle was the one that had loved the rock 'n' roll of the fifties and early sixties. That's where Euell had learned to like it. Tragically, his uncle died less than a year later in a terrible automobile accident.

Euell's reminiscing had been painful in some ways. But, it had brought about a great deal of clarity. He could now draw lines from dot to dot in his life and make sense of the sometimes seemingly senseless. There had not been an in-the-house male parental figure. That's why he adopted his uncle, Dr. Cunningham, Mr. Brighton, and Pastor Wilson. Each of them was a positive roll model to imitate. There had been a very negative female figure in his life. His mother had always aborted her duties. That's why he had not dated girls in high school, and the primary reason he had not thought of Mandy as anything more than a friend like John. But, according to Euell's new understanding of himself and his feelings, Mandy was definitely more than a friend to him now.

Euell had begun to realize that no accomplishment of his would ever win his mother's love and respect. If he worked multiple jobs and graduated college nothing would ever change. But, being a workaholic was the one thing that he had used for some time as a curative to his pain. It numbed him as nothing else could, and it was a lot safer and more respectable than alcohol or drugs.

Chapter 20

Mandy's Return

The day finally came when Mandy was back in the U.S.A., and Euell's seemingly endless wait was over. As a result, his emotions were a composite of all that he had experienced, thought, philosophized, pondered, and planned to say to her at the earliest opportunity. Now he wasn't so sure that he could say all that he wanted to say in a coherent, cogent way.

As Euell paced back and forth, he prayed that God would direct his conversation, keep him calm, and allow him to say what he wished to say properly. This was still his prayer as he picked up the telephone and dialed the number.

The phone rang once, twice, a third time, and a forth time. Euell started to hang up when he heard a voice from what seemed long ago say, "Hello."

"Hello to you too!" Euell exclaimed excitedly.

"Euell?"

"Yes. I have been waiting for your return so that I could call and talk with you. There's so much that I want to tell you. But, that will wait until you tell me about Europe."

"Oh, it was great! I would like to return after college graduation. We saw cities, the countryside, castles, museums, cathedrals, country churches, historic sites, monuments, memorials, the rich, the poor, cemeteries, fortified cities, hillside communities, plays, famous shopping districts, beautiful hotels, restaurants of all kinds, all the pageantry you can imagine, and so much more."

"It sounds exciting. What was your favorite place?"

"That's a difficult question to answer. But, I guess it would be the Vatican. The buildings house a wealth of art and artifacts that are astounding. But, the whole time I was gone I worried about you. I knew that you had some plans but lacked a definite place to stay. Your lack of a reliable source of income concerned me greatly."

"Well, I camped out for awhile. It was an experience I will always remember. I eventually got a job teaching karate, self defense, softball, guitar, and saxophone."

"That's a lot of employers. How do you get from job to job?"

"Well, my transportation is a good, used bicycle. But, I don't have to travel from one job to another. I teach all of the classes at Community Youth Center. I've been very fortunate in that regard, and in the fact that I have made some friends."

"Who is she?" Mandy asked jokingly.

"It's not as much a 'she' as it is a 'they.'"

"Oh, so you want to rub it in, do you?"

"No. Actually the friends are male. I told you all about them in my many letters to you. But, I'm sure you haven't had the time to read them yet. One of the friends is a professor. Another is my temporary landlord. And, my minister is the third. They have helped me a great deal."

"So things haven't been so bad?"

"I won't go so far as to admit that! Some other time I'll tell you the details of my trials and tribulations. But, the singularly most important thing that happened was based on a dream I had one night."

"Did you dream that you were going to join the French Foreign Legion?"

"Not exactly." Euell hesitated until he had found the right words. "Remember how we met?"

"Of course. How could I ever forget? You tackled me on the street right in front of our principal."

Euell had to laugh at her interpretation of the incident of so long ago. "Well, ever since that time we have been inseparable, except for the European trip and my present 'vacation.' We were so close that I took you for granted. But, when you left for Europe and I left for my wilderness wandering, I experienced loneliness I never dreamed possible. Then one night my dreams focused on you. When I awoke, I realized that I have, for some time, had feelings for you that go well beyond friendship." Euell hesitated when he thought that he heard a soft gasp. Then he continued. "I have thought of so many ways to tell you. None of them are adequate. I considered not telling you for fear of rejection. What I'm saying is that I would like to see if you would be willing to go on a date after the first semester. The details can be worked out later. But, the important thing is to get to know each other in a new light. Do you know what I mean?"

"Well, I..."

"Maybe I dumped this on you too suddenly. Maybe you don't think of me romantically at all. But, could we give it a try?"

"A problem is that we both have college in front of us. This could really complicate our lives."

"Or simplify them," Euell said hopefully.

"I don't know what to say. I mean, I kind of thought of us as girl friend and boyfriend a couple of times in the past. And, I really missed you this summer. But, I'm overwhelmed. I can't give you an answer right now."

Euell was emotionally deflated. But he managed to ask, "When, then?"

Mandy seemed suddenly in a hurry. "I have to go right now. Give me your number and I will call you back in a few days."

Euell explained that he was using a pay phone. "If you will tell me when you will be calling I will be here waiting. Or I can call you."

"No, you spent your money on this call. I'll pay for the next one."

Mandy and Euell agreed to a specific day and time that did not interfere with their schedules.

"Good night, Euell. And, thanks for the call."

"Good night, Mandy."

Euell walked away from the telephone with mixed feelings. He felt good about their conversation in general. But, he felt very nervous about Mandy's response to his very mention of a romantic interest. Had he placed too much confidence in a dream?

The phone rang as Euell was only a short distance away. He kept walking. But, suddenly, inexplicably, he felt that he had to answer the phone. What if it was Mandy with an earlier-than-expected call? He turned and ran toward the phone booth, picked up the receiver, and somewhat breathlessly said, "Euell Edwards."

"Euell, I don't have to think it over. I can give you an answer tonight. Right now in fact. I would love to try things out as girl friend and boy friend." That having been said, the two talked of many things they had experienced over the summer months and agreed to keep the previously arranged phone appointment.

As Euell again walked away from the phone booth, he was jubilant. There was a spring in his step that had never been there before. There was a smile on his face that had been rare his entire life. There was a hope he had never known except through God. And, there was a respect for women that he had only recently realized was lacking in his life. His mother, as his primary example, had distorted his view of the feminine gender. Of course his thinking was based on over- generalization. That fact was now becoming crystal clear. Deep down, Euell probably always knew that his mother did not represent the female population to any large extent. But, this particular, rare moment brought clarity. It made him feel significant, loved, and very much alive. Clearly Emerson was right when he said, "When it is dark enough, men see the stars."

Euell's sky had indeed been black. Now it was full of his personal points of light.

Chapter 21

The Fall

The first semester of college is expected to be very challenging. Of course the academic challenge is the most obvious due to the fact that the leap from high school to college can be a very long jump indeed. Living accommodations, roommates, schedules, part-time jobs, self-initiative, planning, and adjusting to a new community all contribute to the realignment of ones life and thought. In Euell's case, the move would involve a change in venue from the nice guest house to the rather drab dorm, day classes at the university, late afternoon teaching at the youth center, two nights per week at the Christian college, and endless hours reading, studying, doing term papers, preparing for tests, taking copious lecture notes, attending church, and staying in touch with his friends.

Mr. Brighton helped Euell move from the little house to the dorm. It did not take the two of them very long to move the few possessions from one place to the other, and to clean up the guest house.

"This will be quite a change for you. And, it will take some adjusting on your part," stated Mr. Brighton.

"I know it will. I really do appreciate all that you have done for me. The house wasn't just a place to stay. It was home. And, your friendship made a difference in my life."

"You are more than welcome. Call or drop by whenever you get a chance. Best wishes in your studies and everything."

Mr. Brighton waved goodbye as he turned and headed toward his car.

The dorm room was much smaller than the guest house, and it lacked the storage space to which Euell had quickly become accustomed. Fortunately, Euell was allowed to store his guitar, saxophone, and a few other items at the youth center.

After a few attempts at arranging his things in a neat and useful way, he realized that he would have to get used to pulling some things out in order to get to other items. But, such is life.

The desk held a single lamp that was adequate for illumination needs relative to reading or typing. Additional lamps were placed at the head of each of the two beds. Between the bed and the wall was just enough room for Euell's bicycle. Nothing was as yet displayed on the walls, and the other closet was empty, as evidenced by the open doors.

Euell rested for thirty minutes or so and headed off to work. There was quite a lot of traffic congestion all around the school. Students were moving into the dorms, familiarizing themselves with the campus, or taking care of last minute paperwork.

As Euell was exiting the parking lot and entering the street, there was a blur of motion as a speeding car entered the lot on the wrong side of the driveway. Euell pulled to the right as hard as he could and struck the curb at a precarious angle, resulting in his being catapulted from the bike. He struck the sidewalk with enough force that he was certain that he had some major injuries.

A number of people hurried on past the injured student. But, several students and a campus policeman quickly came to Euell's aid.

"Are you all right?" asked one of the students as she kneeled down next to Euell and gave him a quick visual check for broken bones, lacerations, abrasions, or contusions.

"I'm not sure," Euell replied weakly.

The campus police officer knelt next to Euell and felt for the same kinds of things for which the student had visually checked. He felt Euell's right arm after noticing that Euell was paying it an inordinate amount of attention, especially in the elbow area.

"I'll get someone from the campus medical center," the officer said as he started to make the call.

"I think I'm all right now," Euell said as he stood up on weak legs. He was visibly shaken by the ordeal, but not seriously injured. Even his bicycle and clothing had survived the trauma. He looked a bit dirty and unkempt.

"What's your name, dorm number, and room number?" inquired the officer as he held a pad and prepared to take down the pertinent information. After Euell answered his questions the officer said, "I will try to find that car. It's likely on one of our parking lots. There will be a written report available for you to use for insurance purposes, or for any medical treatment you may later receive on campus. Here's the phone number for security, and the one for the Medi-Center. I'm certain that we will issue a citation to the driver of the car. Can I help you back to your dorm or some other destination?"

"No. But, thanks for the help and for the offer. I have to get to work before I'm late."

The group of good citizens watched Euell as he mounted his bike and headed off to the job site. Several of them wished him well and Euell thanked them for their assistance and concern.

The class assignment for the day was guitar. When Euell arrived, the students had been tuning their guitars and practicing bits and pieces of material that Euell and taught them. But, they stopped their practicing when they saw his disheveled appearance.

"What happened to you?" asked one of the concerned students.

"Some reckless driver almost ran over me in the university parking lot. The car missed me, but I didn't miss the curb. I'm all right, as far as I can tell. Well, tonight I'm going to introduce what some guitarists call 'split chords'. These are useful for blues, rock 'n' roll, and some of the modern country songs you no doubt have heard on the radio or on television. The easiest way to learn the concept and technique is to learn these in the open string position for one string with fingering in frets two, four, and five on the string just under the one being played in the open position. Let me show you what I mean."

Euell removed his guitar from the cabinet and demonstrated the technique for a few minutes so that the students could get a clear visual concept of what they would be doing momentarily. He played variants of the blues style in order to keep their attention on the fret board.

Euell started with a blues progression using A, D, A, D, A, E, D, A, E. "You should notice as I am playing this chord progression, that I am following the blues progression each time through. Each time through is a verse. Now I will simplify the song by concentrating on one chord. I will play the 'A' cord over and over to demonstrate the fingering. You will notice that I am playing two strings at a time. For the 'A' chord I pluck the fifth string open, while at the same time fingering with first finger on the fourth string in the second fret for two beats. The third finger goes on the fourth string, fourth fret for two beats. The little finger goes on the fourth string, fret five for two beats. And, the third finger goes on the fourth string, fourth fret for two beats. We will practice just this segment for some time before trying to go through chord changes. One, two..."

The students tried their best to stay with Euell as they practiced the one chord for roughly fifteen minutes.

"Now notice the various ways in which to play the 'A' chord in a split chord, rhythm and blues or rockin' rhythm fashion. I can play in the fifth fret, using the fifth and sixth strings. But, the finger stretch to do a typical Chuck Berry chord in this fret requires using a finger to hold down an additional string that the guitar nut held as an open string in the practice we just went through. Notice that the stretch is now very long. The way I am teaching the chord is the simple way for now. Later, we will work on the stretch."

The rest of the session focused on the chord progression and timing. Euell noticed that some of the chords were not clear. "If your sound is not as clear as mine, you are either not pressing the string hard enough, you are on the metal fret, or you are slightly touching one of the strings with one of your other fingers."

When Euell got back to his dorm he planned to call Mandy, write some letters, and get to bed early. He was rather sore from the injuries. But, as he opened the door to his dorm room he saw luggage and all kinds of personal items all over the room, and piled high on his bed. Before he could close the door behind him, a brash, young student stepped into the room.

"I guess I'm your new room mate," he stated in a matter-of-fact way. "Name's Grinch. That's what everybody calls me."

"Euell Edwards," was the somewhat surprised reply.

"Hey, can you believe it? I was pulling into lot number five when some lame bike rider almost hit the side of my car with his bicycle. The guy had to be able to see that I was in a big hurry. Lame, huh?"

"Well, actually I was on my way to work and saw the whole thing," Euell replied.

"Then you can vouch for me that this dude was in my space?"

"I don't think that I can. I was close enough to see things very clearly. In fact, I was the 'dude', as you say, that you almost ran over! The incident almost made me late for work, and I still may have to see a doctor to determine if there are any serious injuries."

Grinch's face contorted somewhat as he took a step backward. "You're the dude?" he asked incredulously. "Like, what are the chances?"

The timing could not have been better if it had been planned. There was a knock at the partially open door and the campus police officer stepped into the room.

"Looks like I arrived just in time," the officer said as he looked first at Euell, and then fastened his gaze on Grinch. "I had no earthly idea that it was your room mate that almost ran you down."

"Nor did I," replied Euell. "We had not formally met until this very moment."

"I guess you will want my things off your bed?" asked Grinch in a caught-in-the-act kind of attitude.

"I think that would be a great idea," Euell stated emphatically.

Chapter 22

The Roommate from Hell

T he campus policeman spoke with Grinch in private for quite some time. But, Euell could hear bits and pieces of the conversation. Grinch had a lot of excuses, but no substantial, logical reasons for his reckless abandon earlier that day. The officer wrote his report as the discussion progressed. He wrote out a ticket and handed it to Grinch as he warned him of any further problems. When he finished with the guilty party, he spoke with the victim in private. He explained what had just transpired and suggested that Euell request a new room assignment or ask that Grinch be reassigned.

Euell looked concerned. "I don't want to make waves my first day on campus. That makes me look like a trouble maker."

"Believe me, it will not look bad on your part. The plain and simple truth is that there are troublemakers and there are those who are troubled by them. You are the latter of the two. There will be a detailed report kept on record in case we need to use it for anything in the future. I will keep an eye on things. And, I'll be seeing you around campus. Best wishes for a better day tomorrow."

"Thanks for all your help," Euell said sincerely as the officer walked away.

Euell began writing his letters to friends back home. Immediately, Grinch cranked up his rap music. It was loud, raunchy, and completely distracting. But, Euell was determined to get through the ordeal without an argument or having to call security. He went into the bathroom and tore off some toilet paper, wadded up two pieces, stuffed them into his ears, and returned to the room. But, the noise proved to be too much of a nuisance. The lyrics corroborated Euell's notion that rap (music?) was performed by those with nothing to say and no appropriate way to say it. In fact, Euell felt that the very name "rap" was actually missing its first letter. Spelled with a "c" seemed more appropriate. So, he picked up his stationary and other materials, walked to a grassy area, found a park bench under a light, and wrote his letters. Of course, the story of Grinch was included. But, any way that he told the story seemed an embellishment, though none was needed or given. To kill some precious time, Euell walked around campus for a while, mailed the letters, and headed for a telephone. Mandy was on his mind and soon to be on the other end of the telephone line.

"Hello. This is Mandy. Is this Euell?"

"How did you know?"

"I could tell by your ring."

"How was your first day?" Euell asked.

"It was better than I expected. I met several really nice people and I got everything moved in and arranged faster than I had expected. Oddly enough, I actually look forward to all the work that will be coming my way."

When Euell told Mandy about his day she was completely surprised. "Maybe you can get a new room assignment as the campus policeman suggested. I don't think this can ever work. Grinch sounds like a very self absorbed and immature person. Frankly, I don't see how he will ever be able to do well in college unless he has a major change in attitude."

"I have to agree with you. For now I will ask for a reassignment and keep a safe distance. I really do not want to have a confrontation with him."

Euell felt much better after having talked with Mandy. As he reflected on his day and his reaction to the situations he felt pretty good. He had not lost his temper and Grinch had gotten a second chance, whether he deserved it or not. Becoming even more introspective, Euell thought about how he had handled negative feelings and experiences when he was younger. He had always searched past geographical places and the thoughts from his past in an attempt to find whatever was missing. But, he usually came up empty handed and as hollow as before. He was going to have to pray and read his Bible more than ever. Perhaps he should, at some point in the near future, talk with Pastor Wilson, Mr. Brighton, and Dr. Cunningham about the things that occupied his thought life and robbed him of much of life's joy.

When Euell returned to the dorm room and opened the door to his new cell, he noticed that Grinch had left some of his things on Euell's bed and that all the lights were left on. Grinch was in bed soundly sleeping. Euell thought about waking him up and having him clean off the bed as he had promised. But, he decided to quietly clean everything off the bed, turn off the lights, and go to bed for as much rest as he could at such a late hour.

The next morning Grinch totally ignored Euell, who in turn followed his example and played the game.

Breakfast was not bad. Euell even had an opportunity to make small talk with some of the other students who spoke of home, degree goals, the number of units each one carried, the career plans under consideration, and expectations for the first few days of the new semester.

Between classes, Euell checked on a change of venue, roomwise. He was promised a change would be made as soon as a room became available.

Euell found the classes to be academically stimulating and exciting. Each professor provided a course syllabus that detailed the direction, content, assignment due dates, and examination dates for the semester. Also included were the professors' office hours. Euell's list of things to do was now indeed long and detailed.

Euell enjoyed teaching the softball class this afternoon even more than the usual. It was a physical break and diversion from the heady task of scholarship. It was also a chance to get a little bit of exercise. But, when the class was over, Euell quickly headed for the university bookstore and then made a quick stop to check for incoming mail. Then, it was on to the Christian college.

The class Euell had enrolled in was the Philosophy of Western Religions. It proved to be a very academically challenging class and among the most interesting courses. The difference in feeling tone between the colleges was obvious. There was a definite spiritual aspect that was missing at the university. The professor opened and closed the session with prayer.

Euell hurried to purchase the textbooks for the class. The bookstore had extended hours to accommodate the evening students. As he headed home he felt very nervous about all of the requirements from both of the colleges. He was also concerned about his roommate problem.

Euell grabbed a bite to eat and quickly headed for his dorm. His room was dark and Grinch was not to be seen. He sat down to quietly study each syllabus and assign priority levels to each class based on the proximity in time and the major due dates. Next, he wrote his own list of things to do. This was a composite of the college classes, his part time job, and all aspects of his life during the current semester. Once this was accomplished, he felt much more confident in his ability to actually make the most of his time. He had been deeply absorbed in the task at hand, including readings and note taking. Suddenly the door was flung open with a resounding bang. In walked Grinch, arm-in-arm with a girl.

"Sorry, roomy. But, you will have to leave for awhile. As you can see, I've got a date tonight."

Euell could not believe what he was actually hearing and seeing. He stood in silence a few moments before he spoke.

"Let me be as clear as I can possibly be and still be civil. This is a shared room until one opens for me. You do not have any right ordering me around. I was doing my college assignments *in my room* when you barged in with a girl on your arm and started shouting orders. I'm not even sure that you are supposed to have a girl in the dorm, much less our room."

"Suit yourself. Stay here if you wish. But, you're going to get an education in sex education if you don't leave right now." The girl laughed at Grinch's "clever" words.

Euell's inclination was to knock Grinch on his rear and send the girl packing. But, he kept his head as he packed everything he needed into one of his boxes. He retrieved his mail from the desk and stuffed it into the box with everything else.

Euell was a pitiful sight as he walked aimlessly around the campus carrying a cardboard box that was overflowing with stuff. But, when he finally calmed down sufficiently, he found the park bench he had previously used and sat down under the light.

Letters took priority. He opened the one from his mother reluctantly. It was the first one she had ever sent him. He could not help but think that his mother must want something from him.

The letter was short and to the point. "Dear Euell, I have

to ask you to come back home. I have no income. I know that you can get a job here at home and support the two of us. Sincerely, Mom."

The letter had the effect of a full thrust kick to the gut. How could things be any worse than this? He had been kicked out of his dorm room by a sleazy roommate, and his mother wanted him to give up his future to come back and support her.

As Euell put the letter back into the box he saw something strange. It was a bottle of hard liquor that he had inadvertently mixed with his things as he had hurriedly packed.

Euell had only tasted liquor once in his entire life. He had not been drawn to strong drink. Tonight that would change.

Chapter 23

Repentance, Solution, and Fists of Fury

Euell stumbled into the dorm at something past midnight and found Grinch alone and asleep. It was a lack of coordination more than revenge that caused a number of things to be bumped and knocked around. But, each of the noises only brought a moan from Grinch and a change in sleeping positions. Eventually, Euell found his way around sufficiently in order to fall into his bed and fall fast asleep.

When Euell awakened the next day he felt sick all over. What had he accomplished? Nothing of positive significance. He had consumed liquor-someone else's at that-wasted his study time, and dishonored God. He stumbled from the bed and looked at his reflection in the mirror. Sure enough, he looked every bit as bad as he felt. Washing his face and cleaning up did not help as much as he had hoped. He left the room with a slam of the door. It was as much from anger toward himself as for Grinch.

As students headed for breakfast, Euell headed for the telephone. He dialed Pastor Wilson's number. "I hate to bother you so early in the morning, but I have some serious problems."

The reply came from a sleepy voice. "Euell, is this you?"

"Yes. Well, somewhat. I really don't feel like myself at all." Then Euell told the pastor about his roommate, his mother's letter, and his very unwise choice of drinking to excess.

"Well, young man, we can find some solutions for the roommate problem and your mother's situation. Let's deal with the drinking first. The Bible says to be filled with the spirit. The problem is that you chose the spirits. You're not the only person on this planet that has made this mistake. But, a wise man will learn from his errors. You fell once. You do not have to fall again."

"But, I feel so guilty!"

"That's as it should be for now. But don't let the guilt drag you down. What did Jesus say to the woman caught in adultery?"

" I know the answer. But, I can't think clearly. You know, my emotions over the situations and all."

"In the eighth chapter of John, verse eleven, Jesus told the woman, 'go, and sin no more'. Also, you should remember the story of the prodigal son who had taken his inheritance and lived a godless life. He came back to an accepting father. In fact, the father ran out to meet him. This was a rather ignoble reaction for a Jewish father to display. The father's love and acceptance was more important than momentary embarrassment. Your heavenly father has just come running to you. His son went through the indignity of the cross so that you will have a place to call home. You made a mistake. But, you are still in God's family."

Euell felt a lot better psychologically/emotionally, and spiritually after his phone conversation with Pastor Wilson. But, he did not feel much better physically. He returned to his room, showered, shaved, grabbed his binder and books, and set off for his first class.

In the next few days he found that it was not at all easy to catch up on the work from the wasted night. But, through tenacity, Euell accomplished the Herculean task.

Euell discussed his problems with Pastor Wilson, Mr. Brighton, and Dr. Cunningham on a number of occasions. Each of them gave Euell good council. So did the scriptures. But, the one problem that seemed to have no solution was that of Mrs. Edward's care. Euell could not take on more work hours. He was spread thin as it was. He would not give up college and his future unless there was no other way possible. A move back home may be good for his mother's economic situation, but, it would be disastrous to his calling, whatever that was, and to his future aid to hurting humanity. He knew that God wanted him in college for now in order to accomplish so many things over a lifetime.

The answer to his dilemma came in a very unexpected way. A letter arrived from Frank. He had heard of Euell's mother's plight and had convinced her to take a job as a secretary at his real estate office. The salary would be sufficient for now, and increase as she showed initiative and the acquisition of the necessary job skills. If she "fell off the wagon" and returned to her drinking binges, Frank would put her into counseling or a rehab program of some kind.

Euell was so excited and grateful that he called Frank immediately and thanked him repeatedly. He also told him about the many experiences, good and bad, that he had recently gone through. Some of the stories had been told in letters previously. But, the situation seemed to require a reiteration of recent events.

Most of the days were going well. The university classes, the afternoon teaching assignments, the Christian college class, the assignments, phone calls, letters, Bible study, and prayer all helped Euell stay busy and avoid Grinch and the dorm room.

One evening Euell arrived at his room at twelve thirty in the morning. The room was a royal mess. Grinch was asleep in his own bed and a girl was sleeping in Euell's bed. Enough was definitely enough! Euell turned on every light in the room and commanded both sleeping miscreants in a loud, booming voice. "Wake up! We are going to have a talk right here, right now!"

Grinch and the girl were visibly irritated over the interruption of their sleep. Never-the-less, they both sat up in bed and took notice.

Turning to the girl, Euell said, "I don't know who you are or why you think you can sleep in my bed without my permission. But, you can not. Get out of my bed this second and on your way to wherever you belong!"

The girl mumbled something incoherent and reluctantly got all of her things together. But, before she could leave, Grinch gained his courage. He jumped from his bed and shouted, "You can't tell her to leave. She's my company. In fact, I'm saying that she will stay. You can go sleep somewhere else as far as I am concerned."

Euell kept his composure and said, "If she does not leave immediately, I *will* call campus police immediately!"

Grinch make the mistake of throwing a wild punch that was meant for Euell's jaw. The attack was answered by an open hand block from Euell's right hand, a follow up back handed technique that landed forcefully on the attacker's right temple, a quick step forward with a knee strike to the groin, and a ferocious shove backwards that took Grinch off his feet and into the wall. At that very moment, the door was forcefully opened by the campus police. The two officers entered and began the process of interrogation to discover the details. They already knew that Grinch was a major troublemaker. The officer who had taken the report the day Euell was run into the curb had asked the other officers to watch out for Euell's safety. Various dorm students had reported Grinch for a number of reasons. This evening students had called in reports of loud party music coming from this very room. Some of the students had tried talking directly to Grinch, but to no avail.

The officers questioned the three principal individuals privately. When they finished they found five other students waiting in the hallway to give their own complaints relative to the self- indulgent behavior exhibited by the Grinch. Each of the students recognized why their noisy neighbor had gotten his rather unique nick name.

At last the room was peaceful and the night was quiet and uneventful. The girl had been sent home. The troublemaker had been taken away. And, Euell finally slept like a log in a physical mess not of his own making.

Chapter 24

Gone is the Grinch, and Real Antagonist

At breakfast the next morning Euell overheard other students discussing the latest news about a student named Grinch. It was reported that he barely had the grades to enroll in the university and that his parents had pulled some strings to get him into the institution. Grinch's intent was to party every night, sleep during the day, show up for a class now and then, and deceive his benefactor parents for as long as he could. There were many rumors as to other things in which Grinch was involved. Many of these were illegal activities. The exact nature of these things was being divulged only to law enforcement officials.

Euell returned to his room to gather his books and other materials. As he entered the room the campus police were going through all of Grinch's things one by one, apparently searching for something in particular. Everything was being bagged. The officer Euell had met as a result of the accident stopped him as he headed out the door and said, "You don't have to worry about your roomy. He won't be coming back."

At one level Euell was greatly relieved. But, at another

level, he felt sorry for anyone who would just throw away his life for wild living. Euell realized that a lack of discipline, values, tenacity, respect for God, and respect for God's creation were all too common almost anywhere one looked.

Euell was early for his first class for the day. This gave him enough time to record some of his thoughts. He wrote, "I have come to understand that I really do not have human antagonists. My enemy, my real antagonist, is Satan, whose purpose is 'as a roaring lion, to walk about, seeking whom he may devour'. Satan can do his dirty work through my mother, bullies at school, the ACLU, the self centered Grinch, or abortionist doctors intent on one more baby-kill before high noon."

The literature class began with a question from the professor. "From which three languages have the most significant literary works been created?"

"English and Spanish," answered one student.

Another student said, "While I agree that English is one, I do not think that Spanish qualifies. I would say English, Russian, and Latin."

The professor said, "Most scholars seem to agree that the world's greatest literature was birthed in the linguistic realm of English, Russian, and Greek. Latin was a good guess. But, it was often simply a redaction of some Greek story. Spanish has had its great literature. One thinks, for example, of *Don Quixote* by Cervantes."

"Wouldn't Hebrew be an appropriate fourth great language of literature?" Euell asked sincerely.

"Well, I suppose that is so if your reference is to the Hebrew Old Testament scriptures. They were largely in the Hebrew, and were great products of the Hebrew mind. But, one thing to factor in to this equation is the sheer number of great works within a particular language group. And, this begs the question of greatness as a product of the language itself, the culture within which the works were created, a combination of the two factors, the universality of the writings, cultural values relative to judging a particular work, the number of copies sold, and the kinds of things like literary devices and style that go into creating a great work of fiction or non-fiction."

Euell continued, "The fact that the Old Testament works were foundational for an understanding of a coming messiah, and that the writings paved the road for the Christian New Testament written in Greek, seems to me to underscore the fact that the glory of the two languages are integral."

"Be that as it may, the Jewish writings are not usually accorded equal footing with such works as those by Sophocles, Dickens, or Dostoevsky."

The professor delved into the various factors that prompted the development of the distinctive genre encapsulated in each of the three languages of great literature.

"Let me clarify literature as a concept. Collectively most anything that is in written form could be considered literature or could be part of a compilation that most would call literature. But, does an automotive repair manual really fit our working definition of literature? It may be well written and serve a good purpose, but is it literature? With this as a working, tentative definition, we move to a focus on those writings with enduring significance that exhibited creative imagination and artistic skill. The form can be poetic or prosaic. For our purposes in this class, the writings will generally be works of fiction. They will be juxtaposed with writings that are factual, expository, or journalistic. And, while this does not rule out works such as *The Education of Henry Adams* or *The Autobiography of Benjamin Franklin,* it does separate the kinds or types into discernible distinctives. One distinctive in the realm of Greek literature is myth. But, how are we to understand the word 'myth'? Is there one definitive meaning of the word?"

Euell spoke up again, "Myth can mean more than one thing. It can refer to that which is purely imaginary, whether person, place, thing, event, or idea."

"Like the Old Testament Creation story?" asked the professor.

"No. That is the application if one has dismissed, a priory, the very possibility of creationism or accepts the story as one of many creation myths that were created to explain what the people of that age could not otherwise explain. But, biblical stories can be myths in the sense that they contain a theme, motif, or character type that may express truths about human existence, human nature, or the human condition."

"Though we may perhaps disagree as to which definition of 'myth' appropriately applies to the Hebrew scriptures relative to a divine creator, you have made a worthy contribution to our understanding of the term as it relates to literature writ large as it were."

When the class session ended Euell was headed out the door. But, the professor gracefully blocked his exit. "Young man, I would like to speak with you for a moment, if you have the time. What is your name?"

"Euell Edwards."

"First, let me say that I appreciated the detailed answers you provided for clarification purposes. Your answers were articulate as well. And, while I am personally thoroughly secular in my philosophical world and life views-my paradigm, if you will-I do allow alternative viewpoints in my classroom."

Euell was visibly relieved, and his whole countenance and posture changed from a rather rigid, defensive stance.

"But, let me caution you. There are some professors in this university that are not as kindly predisposed toward views contrary to their own. Indeed, two that I know well, will castigate you for any evidence of a view that tends to validate Jewish or Christian claims. One of the two professors is so antireligious that he will actually fail you for supporting any kind of religious position as anything other than myth as defined in its everyday, every man's meaning. His primary reason for existence, and for teaching, is to destroy what he calls 'the myth of the divine other'. He bathes in secular waters, swims in antireligious currents, and immerses himself in the unholy secular. So, be extremely careful. I can't, in all good conscience, or as a professional, give you either of the professor's names. Do the research before you sign up for a class. Find out which professors are fair with their students."

Euell was both grateful and concerned at the same time. He appreciated the professor's candor. But, he wasn't certain of his full intentions. And, what kind of institution would allow such an abridgment to freedom of thought? Another way to approach this problem was to discover the names of the intolerant professors, take their classes, debate some of their assertions, and hope for academic integrity when it came time to assign grades. After all, there was an ombudsman on campus.

Chapter 25

Television and the Gospel Truth

Euell did not care to watch much that television had to offer. For one thing, he did not have the time to spend on such luxuries. For another, television programming had degenerated to such a low level that it could hold almost no appeal to anyone with anything that approximated a Christian world and life view. If he needed another reason it would probably be that the liberal view dominated the airwaves. But, in a rare moment of free time, a program caught his eye. Without checking the channel he knew that the station had to be on one of the Christian networks. And, he wondered why PBS didn't show similar conservative educational programs.

The documentary was clearly a pro-life presentation that took an extremely strong stand against partial-birth abortion. The program brought the reality of abortion and its horrors into the home. It was graphic and thoroughly sickening. Yet, it was necessary in order to accurately portray the procedure as the most abhorrent, ungodly, repulsive, barbaric act imaginable. And, while abortion was called into question in general, partial birth abortion was targeted specifically. There were five basic steps to the procedure. First, ultrasound guided the baby- killer abortionist to the baby so that the baby's legs could be clamped by the forceps. Second, the baby's legs were pulled into the birth canal. Third, the abortionist delivered the baby's entire body, except for the head. Fourth, the highly paid executioner jammed scissors into the baby's skull before opening the scissors to enlarge the hole. Fifth, the scissors were removed and a suction catheter was inserted to allow the baby's brains to be sucked out of its skull. This caused the skull to collapse. The final stage was the removal of the dead baby's body.

Euell was so upset and angry about the procedure that he had to sit quietly for quite some time. Once he had calmed down sufficiently, he called Pastor Wilson and explained what he had just witnessed.

"I don't blame you for being upset. Every time I think about the actual procedure for any kind of abortion and the disgraceful litigation that made it legal, I am reminded of Hitler's barbaric acts during World War II. It is as barbaric as anything I can possibly imagine."

"What can we do about this horrible crime against man and God?"

"We can start with keeping partial birth abortion illegal. President George W. Bush signed the ban in 2003. The Supreme Court upheld the ban in 2007. But, angry, militant, extremist liberals are trying to find a back door in order to impose this abhorrent procedure on our nation. The abortion industry stands to lose a lot of money. Perhaps it is time to preach another sermon on this irrepressible topic. In fact, I will change my plans for this Sunday's topic. I want to focus on the overall issue of abortion."

Euell waited the rest of the week in anticipation of the sermon. On Sunday the crowd was a little larger than normal. That was a good thing. There would be more people exposed to the truth. As the song service ended, the pastor took his place behind the pulpit. Euell noticed a more somber, serious expression than was the norm.

"Today's sermon relates to a subject that is crucial to understand, difficult to contemplate, always controversial whether preached or taught, as divisive as all sins tend to be, debated by our representatives, ruled on by our courts, opposed by many physicians, and supported by many liberal groups. I ask you to hear me out, regardless of your personal belief concerning this issue. Even if you have been guilty of this great sin against God and man, you can find forgiveness and restoration. The topic is probably rather obvious to many of you by now. I refer, of course, to the issue of abortion. It is a sermon topic to which I have preached previously. But, most of what I have to say will be materially new.

In Genesis chapter one, verse twenty-seven, we get a glimpse of man's physical beginning. 'So God created man in his own image, in the image of God created he him; male and female created he them.' If you are an evolutionist, theistic evolutionist, or atheist, you no doubt dismiss this scripture as a mythic way to explain that which could not be scientifically explained prior to Charles Darwin's now famous theory of evolution. You may, if you are a theistic evolutionist, postulate a creator God that created all that exists over long periods of time. But, there is the problem of lining evolution up (with or without God) with the second law of thermodynamics as it relates to entropy. The scientific law of non-contradiction clearly indicates that we can not have two opposing laws and at the same time have both be true. One can be true and the other false, or both can be false. But, they can not both be true if they contradict each other. I know that many of you are thinking that I am way off topic. But, wrong thinking in one critical area drastically effects the thinking in other areas that may be directly or indirectly related. This kind of evolutionary thinking led to the God-is-dead ideology, the death of biblical truths, and eventually the death of man as an expediency for the Nazis and others. Though it is unlikely the case that Social Darwinism was planned by the early evolutionists, it was a natural progression of thought that moved from the biological implications of survival of the fittest to the racial, sociological, and philosophic aspects that are almost omnipresent in our culture and that of others in our post modern world.

If a creator-God exists as any kind of reality, and not just as a figment of our imaginations-and many of us know he exists experientially and personally-and if he created us in his image, it is the ultimate presumption to take an innocent life. By whose authority do we commit this foul deed? Is it by the decree of an earthly king, a dictator, a congress, a supreme court, a president, an evolutionist, an atheist, an agnostic, a materialist, a secular humanist, a rationalist, or an abortionist whose hands drip with the blood of his innocent victims? Forbid it, Almighty God!

Pope John Paul II called abortion the defining evil of the twentieth century. And, I believe that it continues to be the defining evil of the twenty-first century. That baby in the womb depends on you, the mother, for its well being. Our creator God gave you that responsibility. And, that precious, innocent, developing little human being that was made in God's image depends on a just society to never allow a criminal or an abortionist to disturb the womb.

There's a song that says, 'I heard the scream of children taken from the womb. I heard Satan laughing by the sacrificial tomb. I saw the wealthy doctors as they hurried through the room, intent on one more baby-kill before high noon.'

That's quite a picture, isn't it? The tortured unborn child is sacrificed to Satan for his pleasure and for parental abrogation for some kind of personal expediency. The doctors are rushing to make the kill and send the bill. But, as the song says, there is a reckoning coming. High noon is nigh. Our nation will not stand guiltlessly before a holy God. Neither will any individual who has not repented of this grievous sin and accepted Jesus as personal Lord and Savior.

Listen to the chorus of the song. 'My name is Justice,

I won't be denied. My name is Truth and you can not hide. I might be hidden by some liberal lie, but my name is Justice, I won't be denied."

You can reject God and all he offers you. You can laugh at his wrath to come. You can say that his grace and mercy will not allow judgment to fall on our nation or on its individuals. If you really believe this lie from Satan, you either have not read the Bible, or you completely misunderstood everything that you read.

Second Chronicles, chapter seven, verse fourteen says, 'If my people who are called by my name will humble themselves and pray and seek my face and turn from their wicked ways, I will hear from heaven and will forgive their sins and heal their land.'

People, Listen! It's not just Satan and his demons working through abortionist 'doctors' and ultra-liberal representatives. It is also the heartless, mindless, godless anti-American ACLU and its bedfellows as well as good men and women who do nothing about this horrible sin against man and God. We are neck deep in spiritual warfare, like it or not. The sixth chapter of Ephesians says that we must gird up our loins with truth, take up the breastplate of righteousness, wear the shoes that are the preparation for the gospel of peace, use the shield of faith, the helmet of salvation, and the sword of the Spirit which is the Word of God.

People, it is time to be counted. Stand up, speak up, and hold the truth up for all to see. Christ had his cross to bear for our salvation. We have our crosses to bear. The world won't like it. But, the world didn't like our savior, Jesus the Christ, either. The world made of him a charlatan, or good teacher who was misunderstood, or simply a prophet, or a delusional man, or a sinner, or a created deity as designed by the apostles after the crucifixion. But, the gospel truth is that he is either your lord/master and savior, or he is not. There is no neutral ground. This is the foundation to understanding ultimate truth, and correlated truths such as the sanctity of life and our God-given responsibility to challenge every attempt to distort the perspicuity and veracity of God's Word.

What we are about to do may be considered by some people to be old fashioned or out of style. But, giving an altar call gives you an opportunity to accept Jesus as your Lord and Savior if you have not done so. It allows you a chance to come back to God if you have been a prodigal son or daughter. It provides an opportunity to come forward signifying that you will stand for righteousness and fight for the defenseless."

As Pastor Wilson bowed his head he prayed, "Lord, forgive us our many sins. May we repent and come to you, as the scriptures clearly require. Heal our land and bless us as we take up our crosses. We will not likely be popular for standing up as the redeemed who are perfectly clothed in your righteousness, ready to fight the fight for your kingdom. Give us the strength, wisdom, and tenacity to do that which you require of all born again believers. Help us remember when the talk-show hosts and others in the media ridicule us, that you are sovereign and that they know not what they do. I ask these things in the name of the Father, the Son, and the Holy Spirit. Amen."

Chapter 26

Life and Constitution 101

After the church service Pastor Wilson was addressing several church members who had inquired as to books and other sources relevant to life in the womb, abortion, the debate over abortion, the court cases that touched on the issue, the biblical perspective, and ways to get involved in right to life organizations or as individuals.

Euell overheard the pastor saying, "I don't know if you have a copy of a booklet called, 'The First Nine Months'. It was published by Focus on the Family in Colorado Springs. The photos were taken from *A Child is Born*, courtesy of Lennart Nilsson."

When the crowds thinned down, Euell told the pastor that the sermon was one of the best that he had ever heard. "If someone takes offense over hearing the truth, so be it. I was once told never to apologize for a life of the heart and mind. But, an apology is always required for heartless, mindless words and deeds."

"Well, there certainly is a great need for Christian political activism. But, it should never take the place of preaching the gospel to a lost and dying world," Pastor Wilson said rather emphatically.

Euell frowned and said, "I've heard of some churches being monitored by members of Americans United for Separation of Church and State. If the spies deem the sermon to be too political, usually meaning partisan or for a particular candidate, they report the information to the Internal Revenue Service. This can actually result in the church losing its tax exempt status."

Reverend Wilson nodded in agreement. "It can indeed lose its tax exemption. And, it's almost always used against conservative churches, though I did hear of one liberal church being challenged. The usual scenario is that of a liberal politicizing in a church and the news media coverage that seldom takes note of the prejudicial double standard."

"I heard the same report about the one liberal church having been turned in to the IRS. I think we would both agree that both conservatives and liberals should be allowed to speak freely on issues and candidates based on their own understanding of the scriptures. Martin Luther King, Jr. certainly spoke to the critical issues of his day."

The minister was looking through a stack of books as he replied, "The first meeting of the House of Burgesses was in a church in Jamestown, Virginia in the year of our Lord, 1619. Government, morality based laws, Christian principals, and English law came together in that setting and formed the foundation of a good working relationship between church and state. Later, during the American Revolution, ministers spoke on issues relating to the rebellion. Many of the preachers spoke passionately about the God-given rights Britain appeared to be denying the American colonists. In fact, there were British leaders who knew of the actions of the patriotic clergy called the Black Regiment. One of these was Rev. Jonas Clark who was over the Minutemen at Lexington. Dr. Samuel Cooper was another member of this distinguished group. In his congregation was John Hancock. In Dr. Cooper's circle of friends were John Adams, Samuel Adams, and Benjamin Franklin. During the long ordeal of slavery in America, many ministers spoke out condemning the wretched institution. Oh, here's the book I was looking for. I have a book mark in the section I want to show you." Turning the book so that Euell could see the various references, the preacher continued, "There are fifty-eight examples of liberals openly campaigning in churches without any problems with the IRS. For example, on November twenty-first, nineteen ninety-two, then Vice President Al Gore campaigned from the pulpit of the Bridge Street A.M.E. Church in Harlem, New York."

Euell looked at the list that chronicled one example after another demonstrating the favoritism of one political party over another. "I have no problem with the exercise of first amendment rights in a religious and political context in a church setting. But, our government must maintain a level playing field."

"Amen to that," replied the pastor. "How would you like to go to lunch with my wife and me? It's our treat."

"I would love to join you for lunch. But, I'll pay for my lunch."

"We'll fight over that later." Seeing his wife nearby he said, "Oh, Martha. Are you ready?"

"I'm ready when you are," she replied.

As the three got into the car and fastened their seat belts, the pastor asked, "Do you have any preferences?" Both Mrs. Wilson and Euell indicated that they had none.

"Well, there's a new restaurant that offers a wide variety of food choices. Why don't we give it a try?"

The ride through the newest section of town was interesting to Euell. He had not had an occasion to visit this area previously.

Parking was a bit difficult to find. But, a parking spot was found within a reasonable walking distance of the restaurant.

The new eating establishment had all the earmarks of newness. Everything sparkled and the employees seemed to be somewhat uncertain of their individual roles. The sign at the front desk read, "Please wait here to be seated." The three hungry people found a seat in the waiting area. As they waited and talked, Euell could not help thinking of the fundamental differences between his mother, Martha Edwards, and the pastor's wife, Martha Wilson. The former was self-centered and anti-Christian. The latter was genuinely interested in other people, and she was definitely Christian in thought and action.

"Wilson, party of three," announced one of the hostesses. "Walk this way, please."

As the trio took their seats the hostess said, "Your waitress will be with you in a few minutes."

"You know, Euell, that the secular world thinks of Christianity in terms of what it opposes. I mean, things like abortion, pornography, drug abuse, alcoholism, foul language, raunchy entertainment, vulgarity, organized crime and not-so-organized crime as well, child abuse, cruelty to animals, murder, rape, incest, spousal abuse of any kind, reckless driving, gambling, and anything that runs counter to the teachings of Christ and the writings of the Old and New Testaments. Many of the unbelievers think in terms of the so-called 'Seven Deadly Sins.' These are anger, sloth, gluttony, pride, envy, greed, and lust. All of these are antithetical to the Christian life. But, I seriously doubt that they could name more that one or two of the positive things we espouse and the things we accomplish in the name of Jesus."

Euell nodded his agreement. "You have a good point. We need to do a better PR job. I mean, the evils have to be dealt with if we want a decent, godly environment. But, the things we support are just as significant. We could begin by changing our terminology. Instead of being anti-abortion, we should say we are pro life. I know that many people already do that. But, that is an example. Another is to say we are pro law instead of saying that we are anti crime."

Martha joined the conversation. "Perhaps we really do need to let people know about the positive side of true Christianity. The seemingly obvious plus of all plusses is that we are trying to reach each person with the life giving message of salvation through Jesus the Christ. But, there are a number of things to which Christians devote their time, effort, and resources. For example, Christians established Harvard College (now called Harvard University) as well as other early American institutions of higher learning; the moral foundations of Western civilization; literacy and education in general; free enterprise; civil liberties; modern science; a Christian civilization beginning with Christopher Columbus; the elevation of women; benevolent organizations; high standards of justice; distinctive art, music, and literature; the civilizing impulse; the sanctity of life; and..."

Mrs. Wilson had been rudely interrupted by the restaurant's manager. "I hate to cut into your conversation, but we have had some complaints from customers concerning offensive religious conversation and we have to politely request that you stop."

"I'm a pastor and this is my wife and our young friend. Just like a good percentage of the people in this restaurant, I'm talking about my career."

"Again, I'm sorry. But, some folks are offended."

"That seems to be the only sin that exists today-being offended. Perhaps the offended ones are much too sensitive about their own lives and much too insensitive about the lives of others. They may be anti-religionists. I'm offended that they are so easily offended, especially in light of the fact that we were speaking so softly. Frankly, I have been regularly offended by vulgar, gutter-mouthed, raunchy conversations emanating from tables near mine in any number of restaurants in the last few years. Perhaps I should have spoken with management and insisted that the offensive speech be stopped. Do you think it would have been efficacious?" Pastor Wilson had passion in his voice. Yet, he kept his voice low and did not "cleanse the temple" by turning the tables over.

"None-the-less, you must limit your conversation to things that do not offend the other customers if you wish to be served. Frankly, religious talk is for the church house, not the restaurant."

"Well, today I have finally met someone who has not the foggiest notion of the meaning of the first amendment rights under the United States Constitution, nor the civility to allow a decent, private, softly spoken conversation to continue without censure. Thank you very much for the lesson in anti-religiosity. We will be leaving now. But, I believe that the American Center for Law and Justice, Alliance Defense Fund, Liberty Council, Thomas More Law Center, and Rutherford Institute will be very interested in this infringement of our Constitutional rights. Have a nice day."

As the three outcast second-class citizens got into the car, Mrs. Wilson said, "Well, I did not expect to be the main course. Now I know what it is like being thrown to the lions. But, I am certain that there is a restaurant somewhere in this town that welcomes the patronage of three very hungry outcast Christians."

Chapter 27

Battle Plans

Pastor Wilson, Euell, Dr. Cunningham, and Mr. Brighton conferred as to the best way to deal with the civil rights abuse the Wilsons and Euell had suffered. They agreed that they would write letters to the various Christian defense organizations.

Dr. Cunningham was rather emphatic when he said, "Well, one thing we know for certain is that any action we take will be challenged by the ACLU. But, I believe we should write detailed, individual letters of opinion to the local newspaper. We could also send the letters to the major news magazines. But, I seriously doubt that the editors of the magazines will publish our conservative, traditional views. The editors are usually very liberal. Bill, you are the most suited for directing the effort. Let's put your skills as an author to good use. And, let us not miss the obvious need to write the corporate office of the offending restaurant."

Euell turned toward Mr. Brighton. "I didn't know that you were an author," he said in a pleased-but-surprised voice.

"I guess that conversation had never come up," Mr. Brighton replied simply. Then addressing the whole group he said, "We need to brainstorm the ideas and all possible outcomes. Corporately, we can put something together that will make a difference."

Pastor Wilson said, "Whatever we write should be enlarged to include the big picture relative to what is happening all across our country. This will no doubt put us in the cross hairs of the American Civil Liberties Union, Americans United for Separation of Church and State, NOW, NARAL, NAMBLA, Southern Poverty Law Center, Pro-Choice America, the national abortion industry and any other organization that is in opposition to mainline, traditional, moral practices. In fact, these organizations have aggressive lawyers who seem to care nothing about the United States Constitution, or our rights under a democratic republican governmental form. We have to be prepared for virtually any eventuality. An extreme liberal with a law degree is as destructive as a tornado in a glass factory. And, just like with the Declaration of Independence, what was signed in ink had to be sealed in blood. Let's pray that this time the blood can be simply a euphemism for tenacious labor."

"Amen to that!" exclaimed Professor Cunningham.

Pastor Wilson continued, "In the first book of Peter, chapter three, verse fifteen, we are told to 'always be ready to give a defense to everyone who asks you a reason for the hope that is in you'. That's precisely what we must do. Our premise is Christ first and foremost, and the documented evidence that

Christian values shaped this nation in unique ways that caused it to grow and prosper like no other. Christian activism is needed more today than ever before. Remember the Moral Majority? Jerry Falwell's recent passing has brought to memory many of the past struggles and victories. But, it has also underscored the fact that we have a long way to go, and that the opposing forces are more active today than at any time in history. Dr. D. James Kennedy's heart attack need not be a set back to the movement. We need to continue to pray for his complete recovery and for his organization to use its infrastructure to forge ahead. This is especially critical since Dr. Kennedy's decision to retire. There will be another at the helm."

Mr. Brighton had listened to the banter for some time before speaking. "Remember when President Bush was addressing senators after the nine-eleven attack? He made a phenomenal point about a well-planned strategy and even used a bit of humor to spice it up. He said, 'When I take action, I'm not going to fire a two million dollar missile at a ten dollar empty tent and hit a camel in the butt. It's going to be decisive." Each of the men smiled and nodded agreement as Mr. Brighton continued. "This must be our strategy as well. We need to work with other faith based organizations, the president, congress, the courts, all levels of government, the news media, churches, Christian professors, and others who support our efforts to restore America to some semblance of integrity and civility. We must keep the ACLU and others on the defensive; check into the possibility of major class action law suits against them for the violation of our civil rights under the Constitution; defy the absurd rulings made by judges from the angry, lunatic, liberal left; protest outside every ACLU office in this country; mail protest letters with tea bags to our representatives as symbolic reminders of the Boston Tea Party; seek an investigation of the ACLU and other like-minded groups as to possible un-American and/or unlawful activities that could be subversive; infiltrate these organizations in order to monitor and gain information; make, distribute, and display posters, billboards, and bumper stickers that expose the ACLU for its bully boy tactics, history of abuses, and attempts to dismantle America as it is in order to create a new nation conceived in the warped minds of heartless, godless, anti-religionists; and send a clear message to the executive and legislative branches as to how they can curtail the ACLU and liberal judges who are mega miles out of the mainstream of American thinking. We definitely need to encourage school districts to return to calling winter break 'Christmas' and spring break 'Easter', to stand firmly for the Pledge of Allegiance in its present form, to teach creationism or intelligent design along with the theory of evolution, and to practice freedom of religious expression by allowing voluntary prayer that includes the mention of God, Jesus, and the Holy Spirit. One of the most important things we can do is promote the production of a series of debates between the ACLU and people of faith who represent their perspectives from the vantage point of law, history, and the Bill of Rights. We need to use television, the Internet, radio, periodicals, and talk shows to educate people as to our heritage and the many challenges to our cherished rights. We need people to personify our cause. We need to pull the plug on the ACLU's use of tax dollars to make war on our values and the Constitution. We need some catchy slogans. We need a database for research and the dissemination of information. We need a think tank. We need a massive march on Washington DC and state capitols to demonstrate peaceful resistance to tyranny, to preserve our God-given liberties, and to show our resolve to restore our nation to its former greatness."

Dr. Cunningham jokingly asked, "Well, Bill, do you have any ideas we can use?" Of course everyone laughed.

"Well, I certainly hope that some of the things I suggested qualify as ideas, half baked as they may be at this stage of the game."

Pastor Wilson said, "All of them qualify. In fact you have offered us a number of great ideas. We have to do something. And, this is how it all begins. As Edmund Burke so eloquently said, 'The only thing necessary for the triumph of evil is for good men to do nothing.' This reminds me, we need to involve the women as well. They will have valuable insight that we might otherwise miss. This was a missing element in the Constitutional Convention. Euell, this whole process will be valuable training for you, regardless of what you choose as a profession. You will learn to qualify and quantify your arguments. You will learn to frame your arguments; choose your words well; anticipate the opposition's next move, argument and counter argument. At the same time you will be practicing Christian charity in a practical, visible, and valuable way. Who knows, you may enjoy the process so much that you will decide to become a professor of Christian apologetics."

"I was thinking about Bill's comprehensive list of strategies and ideas," Professor Cunningham stated. "He is a great catalyst for this kind of thing. And, we need to commit these things to paper so that we will have a basis for further deliberation and expansion."

"I think I can remember the salient points," Euell said confidently. "I will type them and let you review them for errors or omissions."

"Thanks, Euell," the professor said sincerely. "I was thinking of how Billy Graham, whose wife, Ruth, recently passed away, preached so boldly for so many years. He preached on a number of topics that are now considered too controversial. In Canada a minister preaching on the sin of homosexuality can be charged with a hate crime. That actually happened in Sweden and it could happen here if we do not take action. Christians are, in effect, expected to tolerate every ideology that comes down the pike, regardless of how warped, evil, or illogical. Bill Maher has stated that 'Christians and others who are religious suffer from neurological disorders that stop people from thinking'. But, clearly, the same kind of biased verbiage can be said of him, and of those who espouse the most ungodly ideas ever foisted on humanity. Let me explain it this way. Suppose we use the same structure, but replace some of the words. Now it reads, 'Secular humanists, atheists, agnostics, materialists, ACLU-types, evolutionists, ultra liberals, and all anti-religionists suffer from neurological disorders that stop people from thinking.' Clearly, both his statement, and ours are emotional responses to a world and life view that is antithetical to that of the one making the pronouncement. The effort expresses and evokes emotion, yet adds nothing of substantive evidence."

Euell frowned and said, "Well, there goes any free time I may have otherwise had. The issues are too important to simply ignore."

Pastor Wilson quickly responded, "Yes, Son. Evil never sleeps and neither can we. I think that God has some plans for us. It was Albert Einstein who said that the Nazis had silenced the universities and the media and that 'only the church stood squarely across the path of Hitler's campaign for suppressing truth...the church alone has had the courage and persistence to stand for intellectual and moral freedom.' And, we have to remember that we have to have some outside assistance. Prayer and Bible studies are prerequisite for anything we attempt. In the eighteenth century, William Cowper put things into the correct perspective when he stated that 'Satan trembles when he sees the weakest saint upon his knees.'"

Moments later the group heard the news of Dr. D. James Kennedy's passing from this life to life eternal. A pall of sadness covered their remaining time together as they thought of the world's loss. But, they knew that Earth's loss was Heaven's gain.

Chapter 28

Mandy's Surprise

Euell's life was full of all that he could possibly pack into it and still have some time for sleep. But, the Christian activism plans were important enough to him, and for the country, that he felt compelled to squeeze the planning and implementation sessions into his schedule. More free time would be available after the first semester. He was pondering these thoughts and making tentative plans when the phone rang.

"Hello Euell! I have some good news for you," Mandy said excitedly.

"Well, let's see if I can guess what it is. You've graduated with a four year degree after only one semester and you are going to move here and do your graduate studies," replied Euell jokingly.

"How did you know? But, the true story is that Dad said he will pay my airfare and hotel costs so that I can come and visit you when the semester lets out. I will be able to stay for three or four days. How does that sound?"

Euell's heart rate increased dramatically. "It sounds great. In fact it sounds too good to be true. We can actually go out on dates and get to know each other as more than long time friends. I will find out what there is to do around here. I have been too busy to find out. I know that there are some great restaurants. But, I'll see what else looks like fun. I can hardly wait to see you."

"Me too. What I mean is that I am really looking forward to seeing *you*. It has been a very long semester. Oh, it was great as far as the academics go. But, I missed you so much."

"Have you spoken with John recently?" Euell inquired.

"I called him with the good news about my upcoming visit with you. He was thrilled and said that he would love to come and see you as well. Unfortunately, he can not make the trip until after the second semester. And, then it will depend on his finances."

"Well," Euell sighed, "it would be great if he came sooner. But, maybe it is not the best time since you and I are exploring a possible romantic interest. We need time together. That reminds me. Have you been keeping up with your karate skills?"

Mandy half laughed when she asked, "Why? Is your town that rough?"

"No, not really. That is, unless we consider the restaurant manager who threw my pastor, his wife, and me out of her restaurant for talking about God and Christianity. I don't mean to be redundant. I know that I wrote you with all the details about the embarrassing and unfortunate situation."

"Yes, I remember the details. In fact, I shared them with my pastor, the church, and other friends and relatives that I write regularly. Something good has already come out of the incident. You and your mentors have begun a political activism plan and you have already carried out many of the ideas."

"Well, the reason I asked you if you have been practicing your karate is that I would like for you to meet my youth center students, help me teach the class while you are here, and help me demonstrate sparring techniques."

"I have been working out fairly regularly. I will try to squeeze in more time before my trip. That means one more outfit to pack. The ghee, I mean."

"I can't wait to see you," Euell said sincerely. I know I said this only a few moments ago, but the truth is worth repeating more than once."

"I will call you tomorrow with the details concerning the flight and the hotel where I will be staying."

"That sounds good. I should be here by nine thirty tomorrow evening. My night class ends at nine."

"All right. It's a date."

"It actually is."

"Bye, Euell, until tomorrow."

"Bye, Mandy. Oh, and tell your parents thanks for allowing

you to come for a visit and for footing the bill. My mentors and their families will be glad to serve as chaperones."

Euell was elated to say the least. But, there were some logistics to be worked out. He needed transportation. Perhaps he could rent a car. It just didn't seem right some how to expect Mandy to ride around town on the handlebars of the bicycle.

Early the next day Euell told Pastor Wilson, Bill Brighton, and Dr. Cunningham the good news. He also asked each one for advice and ideas as to places to go and things to do in and around the community. Each of the men gave him some suggestions and promised to ask their wives for other possibilities.

The old, empty feelings that Euell had experienced all of his life were diminishing to some extent. The maturity and positive changes were largely due to having been around his three outstanding mentors. Even if his mother had never shown him the love that mothers by nature usually show, God, and God through the mentors, had more than made up for the deficiency. Of course, Mandy's upcoming visit constituted part of the reason for the change in Euell's persona.

The last days of the first semester came at last. They were hectic to say the least. There were term papers to finish and submit, as well as final exams to prepare for and to take. Euell's mind was engaged to be sure. But, the heavy load made the time speed by very quickly. And, Euell knew that the struggles of life make people stronger. If one is born with the silver spoon in his mouth, so to speak, he misses out on most of the planning for the future, working, struggling, suffering setbacks, solving problems, and acquiring the virtue of patience. Differed gratification is the master teacher. Euell knew that this philosophical paradigm ran counter to much of American culture. In fact he had been reading a magazine article about Planned Parenthood's pro-abortion position when an advertisement caught his eye. It was a promotional ad for casinos that taunted the readers to try for the pot of gold by gambling. In fact, the ad stated that more money is spent for gambling in America than for the sum total of all that is spent for movies, DVDs, music, and books. He couldn't help but think that this was a sad commentary about a country that once held to a strict Puritan work ethic.

Pastor Wilson called Euell one evening. "I have a long list of places to go, things to see, and activities in which to participate. This is a composite of Bill's, the Professor's, mine, and each of our wives. We tried to list a variety of wholesome things."

"I appreciate that very much. I'm new at this dating thing. And, the fact that Mandy and I have been friends for so long makes me more than a little nervous."

"Well, a little nervousness is a good thing. It shows that you are concerned enough to think things over. But, I think that this time with Mandy will be good for both of you. You won't be in the old environment and have people expecting the two of you to continue in precisely the same fashion you did when you were in junior high school and high school. It's a chance to really explore your feelings and focus on the question as to whether or not you should consider a life together in holy matrimony. Both of you will need to keep your eyes wide open, be honest with each other, and really pay attention to the way you interact. Oh, one question. Will I get to meet her on this visit?"

"Of course you will. In fact, I plan to introduce her to all of my close friends. That reminds me. I will need a better form of transportation. Do you know where I can rent a car for a decent price?"

"I do indeed. In fact, I can probably get you a discount. What do you want, a red Ferrari Barchetta or a Corvette?"

"Both!" said Euell, jokingly. "Seriously, I just need something that runs well and looks all right."

"I will call my friend and see what he has to offer and at what price."

Euell realized that it is always good to have genuine friends who will go the extra mile for you. This was on his mind as he rode his bike to the rental agency his pastor had recommended. When he arrived he noticed that every one seemed to be watching him through the window. They were still staring when he entered the building.

"I'm sure you are all wondering why I called this meeting," he announced in his best Michael J. Fox voice.

Most of the people kind of smiled and turned back to their business at hand. A little humor had broken the tension.

When Euell reached the counter, he asked a young lady if he could speak with the manager. "Why?" asked the agent. "Are you planning to use your bicycle for collateral on a car rental? I'm just kidding. I saw how you broke the ice. Nicely done. Unfortunately, the manager is presently out of the office on business. Is there something I can do for you?"

"Well, I hope so. I'm Euell Edwards and there is a discounted rental car reserved in my name."

The paperwork didn't take long and the once-over visual inspection of the car completed the transaction. With the bike in the trunk and anticipation in his mind, Euell headed home.

Chapter 29

A String for Cupid's Bow

It felt good to be behind the wheel of a car again. Euell had occasionally driven John's car when they were in high school. He had learned that when John said he was too tired to drive he was actually saying, "Here, Euell. We all know that you don't get a chance to drive very often." In fact, John knew that Euell really enjoyed the opportunity.

Once the bike was unloaded at the dorm, Euell headed for the airport. Finding the right terminal parking lot took longer than he had anticipated. But, he still had an hour before Mandy's flight was due. This gave him a chance to walk around the airport stores. The prices revealed the captive audience aspect as well as something about the unprepared flyers that had not purchased reading material and other things ahead of time. Euell watched people arriving and departing and wondered where each one was going, and the purpose for each ones' trip. Some were saying tearful good byes, while others were purposeful and serious in expression and body language. Others were as excited as if they were on their way to Hawaii.

Euell had become so absorbed in the lives of those around

him that he had not checked the time. When at last he did so, he realized that he was five minutes late for Mandy's scheduled arrival. He walked as fast as his feet would carry him. Some of the passengers had already deplaned and were milling around or meeting family and friends. A sudden knot in the pit of his stomach followed the realization that all of the passengers were now off the plane and Mandy was nowhere to be seen. The panic increased as he wondered if she had changed her mind about coming, if she had changed her flight, if he had written the information down incorrectly, or if he had missed Mandy and had begun the courting experience very poorly by being late. Perhaps Mandy was at the baggage claim section.

Euell was startled when someone tapped him on the shoulder. As he turned to confront the person a familiar voice asked, "Did you almost forget me?"

"No! I could never do that. I'm so very sorry. I was here early and kind of forgot to watch the time as I walked through many of the shops. It was not like the shops were all that interesting. But, many of the people were intriguing. Or, at least my imagination reached into each life and I realized that each one of them had a tale to tell, and a reason for the wanderlust."

"That's all right, Euell. I forgive you."

"You're certainly a beautiful sight to behold. When I couldn't find you I began to think that you had changed your mind about coming to visit."

"I was the third person off the plane and I didn't see you anywhere. So I went to the restroom to clean up and get refreshed from the trip."

"Do you have any luggage?"

"I think you will believe so when you see all that I brought. Maybe we should pick it up. It should be just about ready by now."

As they walked side by side they expressed the fact that it was hard to believe that almost six months had separated them. But, in some ways the time had seemed like years.

The baggage claim area was crowded with people eager to get what was theirs and be on their way. Mandy joined the throng of people and watched diligently for signs of her luggage. "I think that bag is mine," she said as she pointed out a very large piece of luggage. The bag was not easy to retrieve. Euell had to make his way through the crowd and grab the bag before it was out of his reach. "And the two smaller bags coming through the skirt are mine as well."

"I hope this means that you are staying more than three days," Euell said hopefully.

"I really wish that I could. But, Dad said three days."

The two very happy people talked and laughed as they carried Mandy's luggage through the crowd and out to the car.

"Is this your car?"

"It's mine for as long as you are here. I rented it for the occasion."

"I feel sorry for you for having to ride a bike all the time. It must be rough on rainy, cold, or windy days."

"It's really not so bad compared to walking everywhere. I get plenty of exercise and I never have a gas bill or car insurance to pay. Are you hungry?"

"A little. Would it be all right to drop off the luggage first?"

"Sure. I think I can find the hotel from here."

As the two drove to the hotel it seemed that everything in the world was suddenly all right. Unloading the car didn't take very long, so an impromptu walk around the gardens, swimming pool and general facilities allowed a few minutes of quiet solitude. Euell reached out and took Mandy's hand as they strolled around and then headed for the car.

Euell was the first to speak. "I don't know what was wrong with me when we were in junior high and high school. Why didn't I see how beautiful you are? And, the beauty is not just exterior. You are a beautiful person in personality as well."

"It is strange. I always thought of you as a handsome male friend who had saved my life the day we met. But, seldom did I consider any romantic thoughts."

"It is funny how time changes things. And, about lunch, what sounds good to you? Chinese, Italian, Mexican, hamburgers, or something else?"

"Anything. I like most any kind of food, especially when I'm hungry."

"I know a good place. It has every kind of food you can imagine. Well, almost. We can dine inside the restaurant or outside at a tree lined stream with a walking trail."

Euell parked in a scenic area and the two walked the trail to the shops and restaurants. It seemed to both of the young people that the very best of their old relationship and the new romantic feelings had combined to create something really exciting.

The food choices were made quickly and the two sat together eating, talking, reminiscing, and totally immersing themselves in the moment.

"You said that you only have three days. So we have today, Sunday, and Monday?"

"Yes. My return flight is Monday evening."

"We have a lot to pack into three days. Do you like miniature golf?"

"Sure. But, don't expect too much from me as far as a challenge is concerned."

The miniature golf facility was in full swing when Mandy and Euell arrived. Young children and teenagers were inside playing video games. Others were outside trying to improve their skills in the batting cages.

Neither Mandy or Euell really cared much for the competitive aspect of miniature golf. They both played well. But, their main focus was on each other and enjoying the time together. When the course was completed, the couple walked the few blocks required in order to explore a well known museum. Walking among the great works of art and artifacts was exciting for both of them. They spent much time at some of the pieces as they discussed them in the college language they were acquiring. Other things were observed briefly. Some items were intriguing enough to spend time with and to view from various perspectives. The Dutch and Flemish masters were their favorite paintings.

After the museum experience, a quick stop was made at Euell's dorm.

"I didn't think you could stay in the dorm during the Christmas break," Mandy said as she glanced around the room.

"That is usually the case. But, administration and campus police made an exception for two reasons. First, they felt sorry for me for the major problems I experienced with my roommate. Second, they felt that it wouldn't be a bad thing for someone to kind of look after the facility during the break."

The walking tour of the campus didn't take very long and the two were off on a driving tour of the many places Euell had written Mandy about in his letters and mentioned in their telephone calls.

Evening had come all too quickly. The time had literally flown by. A quick snack and a short drive later found Euell and Mandy at her hotel.

"Would you like to watch television for a while?" asked Mandy as they approached her door.

"I would love to," Euell replied.

The evening was spent watching television and talking. Actually, there was much more talking than television watching. Their interest in each other was becoming crystal clear.

"I hate to cut things short. But, it's after ten and I'm worn out. I guess the flight and all the activities have taken their toll on me. Oh, I almost forgot. I have to make a call home so my parents will know that I arrived, and to tell them how the day went."

"I completely understand. Can I pick you up tomorrow at eight o'clock?"

"Sure. That sounds good."

"Eight in the morning is what I meant."

"Well, I would hope so. Otherwise most of the day would be wasted," Mandy jested.

"We can have breakfast together and lounge around before church. Pastor Wilson and his wife, Martha, are looking forward to meeting you and having lunch together."

"It's a date," Mandy said as she walked Euell to the door. "Good night, Euell. It was a great day and one I will always remember."

"Good night, Mandy. I'll see you in the morning."

As Euell walked to the car, he realized that he was indeed

in love. How could he ever stand to let Mandy go back home? Life is too short to waste precious time. He had always felt like Buddy Holly, in that he was always in a hurry and felt that what ever he accomplished had to be done now or never. Both Buddy and Euell were either programmed that way, or they were intuitive.

Chapter 30

The Gospel and Falling in Love

Euell slept like a log all night. It was fortuitous that he had set the alarm. But, when its sound peeled through the early morning silence, he reached for the phone, picked up the receiver, and said a very sleepy "hello". He had to repeat this greeting several times before realizing that he was talking to a dial tone and that the ringing sound had not gone away.

Once awake, Euell shaved, showered, and dressed as fast as he could. When he arrived at Mandy's hotel he realized that he was too early. As he started to walk away from the door it opened slowly.

"You're early."

"Yeah. I'm sorry. I must have broken a world's record getting ready. I can come back later if you wish."

"No, that's all right. Come on in."

As Euell stepped into the room it was obvious that Mandy had been up and around for some time. She noticed his scrutiny of the room and said, "I slept very well last night and awakened with an eagerness to get ready for the day."

As the love-struck, long-time friends drove to breakfast, Euell pointed out the places he had not the night before.

"I thought I would show you where my local life began. There's the restaurant where I first ate, and where I met Mr. Brighton and Dr. Cunningham."

"Why don't we eat there?" inquired Mandy.

"That's a good idea. I can afford a nicer breakfast than I could back then."

The restaurant was bustling with hungry people dressed for church. Some were fairly obviously dressed for other kinds of activities. But, who knows anymore? Some people dress very casually for church services.

"I remember you," claimed the waitress as she placed napkins, silverware, and water drinks before Mandy and Euell. "You're the young man who lived in a tent on Mr. Barton's farm."

"See, I told you it was all true," Euell said playfully as he turned to face Mandy.

The two watched customers come and go as they discussed so many things. After eating a full breakfast, Euell said to the waitress, "On previous visits I could barely afford a small meal, much less a tip. Perhaps this tip will make up for the past."

"Oh, you don't have to do that. I knew that you were not one of those rich boys and I didn't expect anything."

"I want to do this. Have a great day. Oh, by the way, this is my wife-to-be."

Mandy blushed and the waitress smiled at the couple as they rose out of their seats and left for church.

Sunday School classes were about to begin when Euell pulled into the parking lot. A quick exit was made and the couple walked briskly to the college and career class.

When the opportunity presented itself, Euell introduced Mandy. "This is my fiancee, Mandy Lassiter." Mandy did not blush to as great a degree as before. Each of the class members introduced themselves one by one. The teacher took care of odds and ends, and then taught a class on the topic of applied Christianity. Between Sunday School and church service Euell looked for Pastor Wilson. He introduced Mandy and Pastor Wilson in the foyer.

"Euell, you failed to tell me that she is such a beautiful young lady."

"I thought that was understood," replied Euell with a smile and a sheepish glance at Mandy. She was again blushing.

The song service was very much like the one back home. Mandy noticed the similarities and whispered her approval to Euell. This was followed by prayer and the sermon. The topic of Pastor Wilson's message was "Old Testament Messianic Prophesies." Isaiah fifty-three was the centerpiece regarding the kind of messiah Jesus would be. What could take several hours to explain in detail was succinctly and brilliantly presented in forty minutes regarding evidence of God's plan prophesied and culminated.

At the end of the service the pastor tried to shake hands with every church member and visitor. Meanwhile, Mrs. Wilson talked with Mandy and Euell. "So, Mandy, will you be able to stay for the week?"

"No. I wish I could. But, my parents paid for the trip and set the limits. I have to fly out tomorrow evening. Euell and I are trying to do a week's worth of sightseeing and all sorts of things in three days."

"Well, I am impressed that you chose church instead of something else. It speaks well of both you and Euell. Would you like to go to lunch?"

Euell and Mandy eagerly accepted the invitation. Euell said, "The only stipulation is that I pay the bill this time."

"Well, you can pay for yours and Mandy's if you wish. But, my husband will not let me take lunch money from a college student."

The two of them laughed, along with Mrs. Wilson, at her humor as they joined the pastor. Her husband was also in a humorous mood as he reflected on the past dining experience. "Should we do an encore of our controversial discussion in what Euell and I call 'Pagan Place'?"

"Well, I do believe that management has learned a valuable lesson in civility and civil rights as well. The Christian law firm that wrote letters in our behalf made the point as to the unconstitutionality of their actions. But, I wouldn't want to push my luck, if that's what I should call it," stated Euell somewhat emphatically.

The two couples decided to eat at a popular buffet that was frequented by church crowds. The line was long, but the food was worth the wait.

"I think we can speak openly about Christ, Christianity, theology, and all things religious without fear of censure," Mrs. Wilson said as she looked at the Christian gathering.

"Mandy, I hear that you are responsible for asking Euell to go to church and then becoming a born again Christian," stated Pastor Wilson admiringly.

"I invited him, he attended, and you can see the results today. He often tells me he wishes he had won a scholarship to a Christian college instead of a secular institution. He enjoys the atmosphere and subjects much more."

"And, with good reason," Mrs. Wilson interjected. "Euell has so encouraged my husband that he has decided to earn his Ph.D. in theology."

The pastor explained, "Years ago I earned a masters degree. I couldn't really afford to continue in seminary at that point in time. And, when I moved to this community there were only secular institutions and one small Bible College that offered nothing beyond the bachelors' degree. But, with Euell's interest, and the fact that he introduced me to Dr. Cunningham, I have decided that there is no reason not to enroll. The only thing that really frightens me is the writing of the doctoral dissertation. I have known of many people who started, but never finished the dissertation phase."

"I hate to change the subject. But, I was wondering what activities you two have done so far," Mrs. Wilson said inquisitively.

The rest of the protracted meal was taken with details of all Euell and Mandy had experienced all day Saturday and before church Sunday. The Wilsons suggested a number of places Mandy and Euell could go Sunday afternoon.

As Euell and Mandy set off on their own, they decided to change clothes and go for a hike in the hills. Sandwiches and soft drinks were packed for dinner.

The drive was a nice getaway. But, the hike was even better. As Euell, Mandy, and nature became one without losing their distinctives, a whole new world opened up before their very eyes. They breathed-in God's creation as they gazed at the grandeur of their chosen environment. They raced up and down some areas and walked hand in hand in others. God's gift of life was being played out as two of God's children experienced the agape gift that was a communicable attribute from the creator. This Garden of Eden setting was ideally situated to allow the godly interaction among Mandy, Euell, and their creator, the gracious sustainer of life, and its multiplicity of blessings.

The day was culminated by Mandy and Euell sitting side by side on an imposing rock watching the sunset. The walk back to the car and the drive home were reflective. The sandwiches were finally consumed back at the hotel. And, as Euell left for his dorm, he kissed Mandy for the first time.

Chapter 31

The Last Day

Both Mandy and Euell set their clocks for a wake up at four in the morning hours in order to make the most of their last day together. So Euell arrived at five o'clock as planned, and met a wide-awake, ready-for-the-day Mandy.

"I can not believe that this is my last day," Mandy stated sadly. "We have done so much in such a short time. That may help compensate for the lack of more time. I didn't say that very well. What I mean is that we have had quality time together and I think we understand so much more about each other than we did previously. Don't you agree?"

"I couldn't agree more. And, I don't want today to end."

Finding a twenty-four hour restaurant kick-started the day. After breakfast, Euell drove to a new park. The two of them walked around the park holding hands and talking. Later they swung on a swing set until time to leave for their appointment with the Cunninghams and Brightons.

"When you come back for a visit, I would love to invite my friends to have a picnic in this park. We could make a day of it," Euell said hopefully.

"That would be nice. And, it's possible that my parents will want to come with me next time."

Mandy was taken to the Brighton's residence where she met the Brightons and the Cunninghams. She could tell immediately that the families loved Euell, and she knew that they had been a good influence on him.

"Would you like to see where Euell lived after the field experience, and before the dorm?" asked Mr. Brighton.

"I would love to see the home that Euell spoke of so highly."

The whole group walked and talked as they made their way from the main house to the guest house.

"The student who rented from us this semester has decided not to return next semester. So the house is empty and available again. And, we just got it all cleaned up again. It would make a very nice home for a newlywed couple," Mrs. Brighton said as Mr. Brighton unlocked and opened the door. The house appeared to Mandy just as Euell had described in his letters. His words had been vivid snap shots that had helped her feel that she really knew the place prior to ever having set foot on the actual property.

"Mandy, I think there was a not-too-subtle hint in what Mrs. Brighton just said. I would jump at the chance to live here again if the situation presented itself. Oh, while we are all together I wanted to suggest something. Mandy and I spent some time in the new park this morning. And, I was thinking that on her next visit it would be nice if all of us could have an all-day picnic with games and activities and such." Euell's enthusiasm was evident to all that were present.

Mrs. Cunningham was the first to react to the suggestion. "I think we would all love to spend the day with you two and your friends."

The others agreed that the idea was a good one, and that they would plan everything in great detail.

The hour and one half visit had not been enough. But, a busy schedule necessitated moving on to the next thing on the agenda. Everyone said their good-byes and wished Mandy well as the two set out on the road again.

"Where are we going first?" Mandy inquired.

"To the go cart track, of course!" Euell exclaimed.

"Do you remember the time our church group went to the cart track?"

"I certainly do! That is precisely the reason I chose this place. I remember how much you enjoyed racing everyone that evening. I also recall that you were a good driver."

The particular racetrack that Euell had selected was actually two racetracks. One was for children and the other was for adults.

"Which track do you want to race on?" Euell asked jokingly.

"And what do you think?" Mandy asked in a humorous way.

Once the two were strapped in and sitting at the staging lights, Euell looked over at Mandy and winked. "I'll wait for you at the finish line."

"Not if I can help it," she insisted.

The light turned green and the carts thrust forward at full throttle. They were running at a dead heat until the first corner put Euell in the lead. But, the next corner put Mandy in the lead. The lead position vacillated until the finish line was clearly in sight. Mandy won by the length of two feet.

"I think we should have a rematch," Euell insisted.

"No problem. The result will be the same!"

"Let's trade lanes this time and we'll see."

Euell paid the fee for the second race and found himself at the staging lights again. This time he was in the inside lane for the first turn. As before, the one in the inside lane would take the lead on the turns and the other would fight to gain lost ground.

Both drivers did a much better job the second time around. They knew the track better and they felt more confident. But, as the finish line was getting closer, it was obvious that Mandy would be the winner again.

As the carts were temporarily abandoned in order to pay for a third race, Euell said, "I think my bicycle riding has diminished my driving skills. But, I'm going to be a tougher challenger this time. I can feel change in the wind."

Race number three resulted in Euell winning by mere inches. But, he had a feeling that Mandy had let off the accelerator a couple of times in order to allow him a fighting chance to win the race. In any case, the fourth race resulted in Mandy winning by a cart's length.

"There's only so much losing that I can stand! Are you ready to go somewhere else?"

Mandy knew that Euell was joking about his losses, and that the move to something else had nothing to do with winning or losing. They had simply spent more time on racing than had been planned.

"For the next event. I have chosen a movie. Have you seen *Amazing Grace*? It's the story of William Wilberforce. He became a Christian and fought for years to end the British slave trade and eventually, slavery itself."

Mandy was quick with a response. "I have heard that the story is inspiring. But, it was my understanding that you have already seen it."

Euell smiled and replied, "I have seen it once, and I plan to watch it many more times. But, I've not had the pleasure of your company to enjoy the show and discuss it in depth."

"All right. Let's see *Amazing Grace.* And, I expect a full critique after the show."

Mandy and Euell sat and watched the show together, enjoying both show and company. They left the show excited about the value of one person's perseverance and commitment.

After the movie Euell said, "Think what a great thing it would be for someone to take on a modern cause and see it through to the end. In the eighteen-fifties, Harriet Beecher Stowe exposed the cruelty of slavery and personified the slaves by focusing on a lovable character named Uncle Tom. Many

Americans had not really spent much time thinking about the issue until the book appeared in serial form at first, and later as a complete novel. Perhaps Mr. Brighton could write a book that would do for the unborn what Harriet Beecher Stowe did for the slaves. The horrors of abortion warrant the effort. If I were a better writer and had more time, I would love to attempt such a feat."

Mandy excitedly exclaimed, "That is a fantastic idea! Take the idea to Mr. Brighton and see if you two can corroborate on the project."

On the way to lunch, and all through lunch, the conversation focused on the movie and on various ideas for a pro-life novel.

After a late lunch, Euell took Mandy to the Community Youth Center to show her around and to introduce her to those with whom he worked.

"Oh, I almost forgot. You need your karate ghee if you still want to help teach the class."

"I do," she replied.

"I like the sound of those words," Euell said rather emphatically.

The trip to the hotel to obtain the ghee was a fast one. Mandy grabbed her outfit and the two returned to the youth center as quickly as they could.

"There's a girl's dressing room to the left, and down the hallway," Euell said as he pointed Mandy in the right direction.

"You can bring me your street clothes and I will secure them in my locker."

When Mandy returned, Euell had already dressed for the class. "Here are my things," she said as she handed them to him for temporary storage.

Euell returned to the locker room as some of the boys were getting changed. One of the boys was first to see the feminine clothing in his hand and could not pass up his opportunity. "So, that's what you wear when not teaching karate!"

"Very funny. Actually, I brought these for who ever may lose a sparing match tonight. Of course I'm not serious. The clothes belong to someone you will be meeting in a few minutes."

"I don't know that I want to meet the guy who wears girl's clothing to a dojo," said one of the other students. All the guys got a good laugh.

"We'll see who gets the last laugh," Euell said half threateningly as he made his exit.

The class members assembled for the formal bowing and traditional beginning of the session. This was followed by fifteen minutes of stretching exercises. When the Japanese command to sit was given, all the students reacted in one accord.

"I have a surprise for all of you. Today, we have a quest sensei with us." As Euell said this, some of the boys who were in on the jocularity earlier, tried their best to keep from laughing.   But, any thought of laughter was immediately stifled when Mandy stepped from her temporary hiding place. "This is Mandy Lassiter. She is a long time friend of mine, and my future wife."

The students soon put everything else out of their minds as they got into the workout in earnest. Euell taught basics and basic movements while Mandy walked among the students and made the necessary corrections to their stances, arm-to-wrist angularity, and the intended imaginary target areas for each technique. Soon, Euell asked Mandy to trade jobs so that she could command the group as he evaluated their progress and made corrections.

The next lesson was on katas-a kind of shadow boxing that allows one to practice choreographed moves as a group in the dojo, or as individuals at home. Mandy took one group, and Euell took another.

The final lesson for the evening was on kumite, commonly called sparring. The students began with prescribed sparring, which is kind of like painting by the numbers. Then, they moved to free form sparring.

The lesson ended with the traditional bowing after some discussion about some up coming tournaments.

"I think one of the girls was jealous of me," Mandy stated matter-of-factly.

"I think I know which one. She has had a crush on me for several weeks. I think the crush has almost run its course."

Mandy waited for Euell to bring her street clothes, then went back to the girl's locker room to dress, while Euell changed in the boy's locker room.

The trip back to the hotel was full of mixed emotions. There was joy over the three days together. But, there was sorrow because of the pending departure.

Mandy took a fast shower while Euell sat in front of the television. When she opened the bedroom door, she was carrying a piece of luggage, and the other two pieces were near the door, ready to be picked up for transport.

"I have checked to be certain that I am not leaving anything. So, I guess I am as ready as I will ever be."

Mandy and Euell spoke very little as they drove to the airport. They had to arrive early for security reasons implemented after the 9/11/01 terrorist attack on America. The luggage was examined and checked in with plenty of time to spare.

"Could we get a Coke or something?" asked Mandy, demurely.

"Sure. I know this place fairly well. Actually, my self-guided tour is what made me late last time."

The precious, fleeting moments passed all too quickly. As boarding time was announced, Euell could not contain himself any longer. "Mandy, I love you. Will you marry me?"

"I love you too. And, yes, I will marry you, Euell Edwards. I guess I have to. You have been calling me your fiancee the whole time I have been here."

The two embraced and then Mandy reluctantly walked away from the one she loved more than life itself.

Arrival was definitely more fun than departure.

Chapter 32

Blue Christmas without Mandy

Euell drove back to his dorm room in a state of deep melancholy. His emptiness seemed to have no boundaries. He had experienced these feelings most of his life to varying degrees. His friends in junior high and high school had helped him considerably. So had the church members and the pastor. Euell knew that his new friends, the Wilsons, Cunninghams, and Brightons, as well as those at the youth center, would help him through the rough times. Meanwhile, he would see if he could put in more time at work, do some selective readings in history, theology, constitutional law, apologetics, current events, contemporary issues, art, literature, and music. Perhaps he should begin writing the book he and Mandy had discussed. First, he would speak with Mr. Brighton about all aspects of the writing and publishing process. Whether Euell or Mr. Brighton wrote the story was immaterial. What counted was the end product with its impact on society. What an opportunity to reverse Roe v. Wade.

One of the tough things Euell faced was the return of the rental car. Life had been so much easier with an automobile.

But, life is full of reversals like the move from a very small home to a tent on a farmer's land, or the move from the Brighton's guest house to the college dorm. The most troubling reversal was the companionship of Mandy for three days and the abrupt change when she had to return home for the holidays. Another was the car that was reluctantly returned. It put Euell back on two wheels, peddling his way to the youth center.

As Euell walked from the bike rack to the center, he hoped that he did not look as bad on the outside as he felt on the inside. He stopped at the bulletin board to check for any new listings. There were openings for groundskeepers.

"Good morning, Mrs. Sansum," Euell said in a rather weak, pained, pathetic way.

"Oh, hello, Euell. Are you feeling all right? You look like you are coming down with something."

"Mandy left last night. I'm just depressed. That's all. I was thinking of applying for the temporary position of groundskeeper. I could use the extra money, and I need to keep my mind busy."

"No use filling out the application, Euell. You're hired. We will arrange your schedule around the classes you presently teach."

Euell thanked Mrs. Sansum and left feeling a little better. But, he had no appetite. He rode to the new park and thought about the time he had spent with Mandy and the picnic that they had begun planning for her next visit. This was followed by aimlessly riding around town until time to teach class. After class he practiced softball skills, followed by karate basics, basic movements, katas, and sparring techniques. When he was sufficiently tired he involved himself in things less physically strenuous. The guitar and saxophone practice took up more than an hour and thirty minutes as he tried to strum and blow his blues away.

Euell decided on another bicycle ride. He was tired enough that he had to alternately ride slowly and then walk the bike for a while. He still possessed no appetite.

When Euell got back to his room he made a few calls to friends, both local and back home. He tried several times to call his mother to tell her all about Mandy's visit and the engagement. There was no answer, so he left a short message and wished her well. When he hung the phone up he thought about calling Mandy. As he started to pick up the receiver, the phone rang.

"Hello," Euell said softly and somewhat guardedly.

"Hello to you too. You sound depressed. And, you certainly picked up the phone quickly."

"I was actually reaching for the phone to call you when you called."

"I've been trying to call you for some time now," Mandy replied.

"Well, I phoned John and other friends to tell them about our engagement and to get over this deep depression that began when you left. I tried to call my mother several times and finally left a message. I wanted to save the best call for last."

"That's sweet of you," Mandy said sincerely.

"I have not felt like eating all day. But, on the positive side of things, I got a job as a groundskeeper at the youth center. The hours will be built around my teaching schedule over the holidays. The job will keep me busy, and help financially as well. I miss you so much already."

"I feel the same way. But, there is so much to work out. We are both on scholarships. One of us may have to give up a scholarship to enable us to attend the same school. That would be difficult monetarily. Another option is to marry and just see each other during the school breaks. But, I don't think that either of us want to do that. Another option is to wait until after we graduate from college, or even worse, from graduate school. Neither of us would choose this option. Perhaps we should give up our scholarships, choose a college, and decide on enrolling either full time or part time. Of course we will both have to work at least part time."

Euell was thinking deeply about the options Mandy had mentioned and considering other viable choices that may not have been considered. "There is no easy solution as far as I can tell. I guess that's the way life usually is for most people. But, there is one thing I know for certain. I can not live without you."

"Those are my feelings exactly," Mandy replied.

The two spoke for some time about becoming one in holy matrimony. They decided that their hometown would be the best location. The date would be set so that their student friends and professor friends, ministers, and others could attend. It was also decided to ask both of their minister friends to officiate.

"I want to talk with you every day," Euell said plaintively.

"There is no reason why we can't. I will get a phone card with free minutes so that we aren't out a fortune," Mandy quickly offered.

"We could e-mail each other daily. But, it just isn't the same as actually talking with each other. Well, I should let you go for now. I'll call you tomorrow night. I love you."

"I bet I love you more," Mandy insisted.

Both said their good-byes and hung up their lifeline. They both had hope for the future coupled with the present hollow feelings of loneliness and depression.

Euell worked through Christmas Break, or Winter Break, as the university insisted on calling it. This gave him the extra money he needed to purchase gifts for his friends, mother, and of course Mandy. It also helped him pay his share of the phone bills for the many phone calls.

One evening Euell went to the Cunningham residence and joined them in watching the classic Christmas movie, *It's a Wonderful Life.*

When the movie ended the conversation began. Dr. Cunningham turned toward Euell and said, "I couldn't help noticing a tear in your eyes several times during the movie."

"It must be allergies," Euell explained weakly.

"Yes, I know. I have the same kind of allergies every time I watch that movie. It yanks at your heartstrings like few movies can. I may be a professor with some head knowledge, but I still have a heart for people and compassion for the human condition. I actually try to pattern my life after the best traits of George Bailey. And, I try to avoid the pitfalls he didn't. Of course the best way to live the life of George Bailey is to live the life Christ intends for his followers. So, don't be ashamed to shed a tear now and then. It shows that you are human and that you have feelings and compassion. These are things that are woefully lacking in our world today."

Mrs. Cunningham offered Euell and Dr. Cunningham a choice of coffee, hot chocolate, or soft drinks and said, "Frankly, I would be concerned if either of you failed to show some emotion over the movie. It kind of reaches us where we live and in ways we seem to forget the rest of the year. And, it is certainly antithetical to all that garbage so many people watch on television in our day. Excuse my bluntness, but television seems to be all about the fist and the groin. It's what I call fist and groin entertainment. One minute there's a fight scene. The next minute two strangers are having sex. Entertainment should center on the heart and the mind. And it can be of neither if it is godless."

"Well stated!" Dr. Cunningham said emphatically.

As the evening grew later the discussions touched on all kinds of subjects. This birthed in Euell's mind the idea that he should indeed research the professors who so vehemently opposed Christianity and Christian ethics. The research would not be for the purpose of avoiding the classes, but for enrolling in order to be the salt the world so desperately needed, as well as to learn practical Christian apologetics experientially. The defense of the faith seemed to be the best way to get fellow students to consider Jesus and to perhaps persuade anti-Christian, anti-Jesus professors to be more tolerant of people of faith. But, battles are seldom easy, nor as short as one would perhaps anticipate.

Chapter 33

The Second Semester and a Thing Called
Academic Freedom

The new semester arrived and things were somewhat back to normal. Euell still taught for the Community Youth Center. The groundskeeper job was put aside until the next summer. There was no lack of things that had to be done. Euell carried eighteen units at the university and five at the Christian college; helped Pastor Wilson, Mr. Brighton, and Dr. Cunningham with political activism for moral and Christian causes; made time for prayer, Bible study, letters, calls, church activities, as well as practice and enrichment in the areas related to his youth center job.

At one of the activist meetings Euell mentioned his idea about writing a pro-life, right to life novel. He even suggested that Mr. Brighton might consider taking on the job. The members of the group agreed that the need was great and so was the idea.

"But," Mr. Brighton suggested politely, "you need to be the author. The idea was yours. You have the ability to write the story. We can all give you some help by way of ideas, components, direction, literary ideas, as well as grammar and style."

"If I begin this very moment, the book may never be written. I have a full platter, so to speak."

Pastor Wilson, now enrolled in his doctoral program said, "We all have more to do than we can reasonably expect to finish. But, over time we manage to get the most significant things done if we are diligent in our efforts and careful with our time. It was the Puritan work ethic that helped create a society built on Christ's foundation. What was begun, we must finish. Frankly, I'm concerned for our nation. As it becomes more and more anti-Christian, neo-pagan, secular humanistic, and socialistic, there will be little chance of writing, publishing, and distributing wholesome, Christian materials. We are already on a very slippery slope."

As the session ended, Euell made a commitment to writing the book on behalf of the precious, innocent, unborn children that were being denied the God-given right to life. Euell knew that his own life had to mean something. It had to be used to make a difference for the glory of God and for the very lives of the unborn made in God's image. He knew the arguments used by the abortionists who preferred to be called pro-choice advocates. And he knew that their arguments were largely designed to hide the real reasons for abortion. These included the greed of the abortionist doctors, the convenience of the parents, and the desire to avoid embarrassment over a birth out of wedlock. But, the embarrassment factor was less and less likely to be a causal factor because of the reprogramming of American values by the likes of Jerry Springer and his clones.

Euell's classes at the university were back in session. But, the third meeting of his history class was a watershed moment. The session began as one would expect. The professor wrote a brief outline on the board, the students copied it quickly, and the lecture began in earnest with an analysis of ideologies and paradigms relevant to the formation of the colonial and revolutionary American mind.

"We know, for example, that George Washington was a Deist. Failing to understand this fundamental fact leads to a misunderstanding of what he accomplished, why he did so in the first place, and his view of religion's role in the new society. His god was a distant, hands-off kind of deity who did not intervene in human affairs. Why ask this kind of god to intervene in what was essentially a kind of civil war between English governmental leaders and colonial governmental leaders who had become adamant about becoming first class leaders, first class citizens, and subjects to no one, not even an absentee god."

Euell had enjoyed the previous lectures and the organized approach the professor exhibited. Yet, he knew that his time to challenge extreme liberalism had come. But, on his mind was the fact that the instructor had failed some students for their adherence to Christian ideology despite the fact that the students had backed up their assertions with documentation.

It was well known around campus that the professor referred to himself as "The foremost evangelical atheist on staff".

Euell politely spoke up. "Could I interject some thoughts along this line of thinking? The older textbooks labeled Washington as an Anglican prior to the American Revolution and an Episcopalian after the war. The transition seems logical. The Church of England would not be able to continue in the newly liberated nation. Its American equivalent, minus official governmental status, would continue to exist and practice the liturgical aspects minus the political. There would be no taxation of the people to support the church."

The professor was visibly irritated. His retort was, "Those older textbooks simply passed down an error begun long before. A careful study of the subject clearly reveals that George Washington's religious beliefs are as mythical as his cutting down the cherry tree or his amazing silver dollar toss."

"Are you familiar with Peter A. Lillback's book entitled, *George Washington's Sacred Fire?*"

"Of course I am, young man. But, we should be very suspicious of any book that is written by a person who obviously has an ax to grind, so-to-speak. The author is a seminary president and a church pastor. His collaborator, Jerry Newcombe, is a producer of the Coral Ridge Hour and a Christian author. What other conclusions would one expect from their collaboration than the notion that our first president was a Christian and that, therefore this is a Christian nation?"

Euell noticed a definite uneasiness among the class members. The lines were being drawn. Some students nodded in agreement with the professor. Some seemed to be appalled that anything of a religious nature, particularly of a Christian perspective, would be brought up in a secular academic setting. Other students seemed to agree with Euell. But, their silence was deafening.

Euell said, "I agree that the author has an ax to grind. I suspect that is the case with most authors. But, the fact is that the ax in question was used to cut away the dead trees that had begun to hide the live forest. The author and his collaborator wrote a book that is almost twelve hundred pages in length in its soft cover edition. Primary source documents were used to provide hard evidence to prove that Washington was not a Deist. He had rather lengthy morning and evening prayers. Would a Deist bother with prayer if he believed that God is distant, uncaring, and unresponsive? And, what about Washington's vast knowledge of the Bible, his commitment to Christian missionary work among the Indians, and..."

The professor cut Euell off before he could more completely make his case. "We have discussed this long enough. The clear facts prove that Washington was a Deist. I will expect that exam questions relative to his religious views will clearly be answered accordingly. Anything else will result in a failing grade."

Euell was upset and astounded that the professor's view was forced down the student's throats without so much as a chance to chew on the facts in order to make an informed decision as to what to swallow and what to spit out.

When Euell got a chance between classes, he called Dr. Cunningham and discussed the matter.

"Well, you knew from the start that this particular professor would not accept a Christian world and life view, evidence or not. And, while it is indeed tragic that he does not allow academic freedom or practice intellectual honesty, he may be fair-minded enough not to lower your grade based on one isolated class discussion. The bright spot is that you exercised your right to a different interpretation based on hard evidence. You did this in an open and appropriate manner. If he does use this or anything in the future to assign a lower grade than you believe you earned, you have the right to see the ombudsman."

"Maybe I am in the wrong college. I don't feel that I 'won the debate,'" Euell said in a disappointed tone of voice.

"Come on, Euell, You are a freshman in college while your professor has a Ph.D. in history, seven or more full years of college, and years of teaching experience. Give yourself a break. You spoke up appropriately. You made your points from a recent source that is heavily documented. The problem is his, not yours. There is absolutely nothing for you to be sorry for unless it is the professor who has a lot of knowledge, but lacks the correct interpretation of the data due to preconceived notions."

"I guess you are right. But, why didn't the Christian students and others who are intellectually honest speak up?"

"The obvious reason is the fear factor. The students lack the experience, vocabulary, and maturity to challenge what is obviously a flawed interpretation. And, there is the all important question of a grade."

Euell continued in the class and occasionally raised a question relative to an anti-Christian position for which he had antithetical evidence. He personally liked the professor and thought that he was brilliant and ever so articulate. It was too bad that he had a major blind spot.

When it came time to do a research paper, Euell decided not to push the issue. He chose to write a paper titled, "The Constitutional Application of the Natural Rights Philosophy as Exemplified by the First and Second Amendments".

The term paper was returned with a letter grade of "C". Nothing was marked as to errors in grammar, syntax, factual information, cause and effect relationships, or conclusions considered and reached. The only note was, "Your title was too lengthy".

Dr. Cunningham agreed to review the paper. So did Mr. Brighton. Both agreed that the paper was very strong for the freshman level, and that it was indeed an "A" paper, lengthy title or not.

Euell took the paper to three different professors at the university. All three advised him to speak directly to the professor who had assigned the grade. Only one of the three took the time to actually read the paper. His take on Euell's paper was that it was well crafted, and accurate, and would have gotten an "A" in his class. But, he asked Euell not to disclose their conversation to the professor in question.

Euell waited a couple of days in order to cool down a bit. Then he read the paper as dispassionately as he could. He found a minor error that had not been marked. But, nothing in the paper was significant enough to have brought the paper down to a "C". After one more very careful reading he got up the courage to speak with the professor during his office hours.

Euell found the door open and the professor busy at his computer. He leaned in and knocked on the door. "Do you have a few minutes to discuss my term paper?"

"Only a few. I have a class that starts in ten minutes."

"My question concerns the grade on my term paper. I noticed only one comment on the entire paper. It was concerning the length of the title. Is that one fault sufficient to lower the grade to a 'C'?"

"Well, the title encapsulates the paper's overall contents. If it's faulty, the whole paper is faulty."

"I asked four professors and a published author to read my paper. The author and two of the professors consented. Each of them agreed that it is definitely an 'A' paper."

"Well, I do not agree, and I question the professionalism of other professors who would read your paper and second guess my reasoning relative to the grade. The "C" grade will remain. You still have the final exam. Study hard and you may see the overall grade approach your preconceived expectation. I have a class to teach. Have a good day."

As Euell exited the office he was all but pushed out of the way by the professor's haste to make his escape and arrive on time for his next class session.

A stop at the admissions and records office allowed Euell to obtain information regarding the ombudsman and the process involved. He set up a tentative appointment.

The meeting worried Euell. He wondered what effect it would have on his present classes and the future classes as well. Would the other professors hear of the situation and think he was a troublemaker or a poor student? But, at the last moment Euell decided to keep the appointment. If he canceled, other students would probably suffer the same kind of abuse that he had endured.

"Well, Euell, you have explained all of your concerns in an appropriate manner. I have some options. I can talk with your professor and encourage him to re-read the term paper. But, even if he agrees to read it again, there is no guarantee that he will raise the grade. In fact, he may actually find some reason for which to lower the grade. I can ask him to be fair with you on the final exam and hope that your grade will be raised. Or we can wait and see how the exam turns out, and then go through the process if necessary."

"I guess I will wait for the final exam results. Anything you do in my behalf may jeopardize my overall standing."

"I concur. Just hang in there. Don't let one bad experience ruin your life. Best wishes, and I hope everything works out for you."

Euell studied for the exam until he knew the material thoroughly. This was nothing new. It had always been his habit. On the test day he took the exam and knew that he had aced it. But, he gave honest answers regarding Deism and he documented everything with direct quotes and various interpretations by major historians.

The results were posted by student numbers. Euell had received an "F" for the final exam and an "F" for the semester. It was time to see the ombudsman.

Chapter 34

Judgment and the Arrival

The first year of college was now completed. Euell had earned straight "A's" except for the "F" due to philosophical differences between the professor and student. Their opposing world and life views should never have resulted in a grade less than that which was earned. But, when indoctrination is the main goal in any institution or particular class, there is the possibility of dogmatic interpretations taking priority over scholarship. The professors who understand this and make every effort to be fair, look at the scholarship revealed in the student's term papers and other written materials and judge as to whether or not he or she sufficiently supported major assertions with evidence and logic.

The day finally arrived for possible vindication for Euell's grade. Euell took the formal letter from his mailbox and started to open it immediately. Instead, he decided to wait until he walked back to the dorm, took a letter opener to the envelope, and carefully read each word that could either change his grade or his future. At the end of the letter were signatures of each person who had contributed to the decision. Euell stood in silence after having read the letter a third time. He thought of all the plans and sacrifices he had made in order to go to college and of all the effort he always put into his studies. He thought about the other professors who had been fair with him regardless of their personal predilections relative to his point of view or paradigm. Why should one professor have the power to utterly destroy a student's academic record or force the student to retake the class? Euell was not cut out to be an intellectual clone of anyone else. God had given him a strong mind and a will malleable to God. He knew that he had a right to exercise what God had provided him.

Suddenly the enormity of the decision hit him full force. Even professors had to play by the rules. Euell had been vindicated. The board unanimously agreed that he had earned an "A" in the class and that the work was well above and beyond that of a typical underclassman.

Phone calls had to be made immediately or Euell would explode. Each one who knew of the problem and had supported Euell received a thank- you call and the good news. Most of them admitted that they had been praying for a fair settlement.

The most important call was reserved until last. When Mandy heard the news she said that she was glad that fairness had prevailed. "I'm so proud of you," she said somewhat forcefully. "You stood up for your rights and those of all people of faith. And, you did it properly and without malice."

"I'm just glad it is over. I thought about it night and day. It was my first and last thought each day. I tried to leave it all in God's hands, but I kept worrying about it incessantly. I hope I will do better if there is ever a next time."

"We learn many of the hard lessons through the trials of life. This was just one more lesson in applied Christianity. You know that Jesus never said that being a Christian in thought, word, and deed, would be easy."

"I still think I should have chosen a Christian college," Euell said in a matter-of-fact manner.

"But, that's kind of like going to a monastery. You can benefit to some extent because of the immersion into Christian living. But, you can't really be the salt if you are not where the seasoning is really needed the most. That's a decision you will have to make."

"No. That's a decision *we* will have to make."

"Okay, I'll accept that joint obligation. And, speaking of us, we will be coming your way this Wednesday at 9:45 AM. By 'we' I mean my father, mother, John and his sister and parents, and of course, me. Dad offered to pay your mother's way in full, but she declined the offer. Regardless of that, there will be seven of us to deal with. I can't wait to see you."

"Nor can I wait to see *you*. A rental car is my next order of business."

"You won't have to rent a car this time. Dad said that he will rent one for me to drive. I guess he knows how badly I beat you in the go cart races!"

Euell laughingly replied, "This means a rematch."

"Actually, you can do the driving, or at least some of it. We will add your name to the contract."

Things were looking good. Euell was planning to attend summer school at the Christian college. Mr. Brighton had agreed to let him rent the otherwise empty-for-the-summer guest house. But, for two whole weeks Euell had no obligations at college, the youth center, or anywhere else that he could think of, with the exception of church. With all of this in mind, he quickly moved all of his things to the Brighton's guest house and spent the balance of the day relaxing with his favorite music and contemplating the coming people and events.

Wednesday morning arrived and found Euell up and around at 4 A.M. There was no possible way that he could sleep. He showered, shaved, brushed his teeth, and caught a cab to the airport. Though he was hungry, he was too nervous and excited to eat. To ease the tension, and to have something to do, he alternately walked and sat until he had covered the whole terminal more than once. The time seemed to stand still. Every time he looked at his watch he found that he was only another minute closer to the grand arrival. He pulled a book from his backpack and decided to devote all of his attention to it. The book was a Norton Critical Edition of Thoreau's two most famous works, *Waldon* and "Civil Disobedience".

At long last the arrival of flight number 1107 was announced. Euell bounded to his feet and sprang toward the deplaning area. Close to half of the passengers had off loaded when Euell finally got a glimpse of Mandy's mother. As he watched he saw each of the others who were scheduled to visit. Mandy was the last one in the expected group. Euell's heart felt like it was skipping a beat as he impatiently awaited Mandy's embrace.

"There's Euell," John announced loudly for the benefit of the other six members of the party of seven traveling companions.

Mandy ran past the others and leapt into Euell's waiting arms. Her kiss was soft, swift, loving, and shy. She stepped to his left side as he shook hands with John and his parents, patted John's sister on the head affectionately and commented on how much she had grown since he had last seen her. Mandy's parents would not accept a handshake. They simultaneously hugged Euell as he stood holding Mandy's hand.

Mandy whispered in Euell's ear, "I have missed you so badly."

"I know that feeling all too well," he answered softly. Turning to the group of friends, he asked, "Is anyone hungry yet?" They answered in the negative. "Well, if not, let's get your luggage and get out of here."

Once the luggage was collected, Mandy's father remarked, "I'm glad we decided to rent two cars. Can you imagine trying to fit all of us *and* the luggage into one vehicle?"

"I was able to get you a discount on the cars," Euell stated. "Your reservations were already booked, but I was able to persuade the agent to give you the discount."

"Thanks, Euell. I appreciate it very much," John's father said. Mandy's father chimed in as well.

"Well, that is the least I could do for all you have been through in cost, effort, traveling, and time."

"It is really kind of a visiting vacation and a getaway vacation all in one," John's mother explained.

"I have maps that I have marked for you so that you can see the things that you wish to see while you are here. And, of course I would be glad to be your tour guide if you wish," Euell offered sincerely.

"No he won't," Mandy protested. "I plan to almost totally monopolize his time."

The group carried their baggage to the rental car area. One of the rental cars was a rather large passenger model, and the other was a seven-passenger van. The plan was to get all the luggage to the hotel as soon as possible. Once unloaded, the van would transport the out-of-towners, minus Mandy. She and Euell would drive the other vehicle at least some of the time.

The hotel of choice was the same one that Mandy had stayed in previously. With so many hands on the luggage, the vehicles were emptied quickly and the two rooms became depositories for the travel items. This having been accomplished, the group freshened up. Mandy was the first to finish in order to take a walk around the facilities with Euell.

"I'm so glad you got things straightened out with the university professor. I guess I have been very fortunate. Even though mine is a secular institution just like yours, the professors have been open to various view points as long as I can give evidence for the assertions that I make."

"Perhaps I have been too negative about attending a very secular school. But, I never want to have another experience similar to the one I endured. And, if it occurs again, I hope that I have the courage to stand my ground. The whole thing has been an experience I can learn from and use in some way. But, I'm not sure just how at the present time."

"How's your schedule at the youth center? You weren't certain about time off when last we spoke."

"I'm on an unpaid vacation for two weeks. When I return to work I will be working as a groundskeeper and teaching classes as usual. And, I will be attending summer school at the Christian college. So, I am excited about the two weeks you will be here, the larger salary from the youth center, and the study time I will have for the Christian school. The longer working hours will help occupy my mind and my time when you return home. Unless we elope."

The group was finally ready for lunch. They loaded into the two vehicles and headed out for the buffet they had discussed. It felt like a tour bus had arrived as the party of eight got out of their transport units and descended on the restaurant. The selection of two large tables was made and the food was dished up quickly so that the hungry entourage could say grace and begin devouring the tasty morsels.

"John, tell me about your college," Euell requested.

"Well, it's a large university with an ivy-league look similar to Harvard. The classes are over-crowded in some cases and small numerically in others. Most of my professors are really good. Well, there was one exception. But, I guess there is always that one that doesn't really enjoy teaching any longer."

"I know that I will never forget the atheist professor that insisted that George Washington was a Deist and failed me even though I had research on my side."

"I hope most of the professors are more professional than this one," John said sincerely.

"Oh, I think they are. Many of them disagreed with my paradigm without docking any points as long as I supported my assertions with solid evidence."

"Euell, let's take everyone on a tour of all the places we visited last trip," Mandy pleaded.

"I would be glad to if everyone is interested. The places may not be as interesting to them as they were to us during that special time. But, everyone can learn the lay of the land now in order to get around on their own later."

"I like the idea," John's father said.

Euell took the group to all the places he had told them about in his letters and phone calls. When he stopped in a parking lot or other safe area, the other car would pull along side, and Euell would explain what they were viewing. He made sure to emphasize the things he and Mandy had seen and experienced on her last visit.

"You know, Euell, these places really are somewhat special. But, what made them special was what we felt when we were here before," Mandy said softly, in an introspective moment.

Euell was a little embarrassed by the softly spoken words that he felt certain had been overheard by those in the other car that was parked so close to theirs. Therefore, his reply was even softer. "I know. And, we should definitely revisit each one."

Once the tour was over, so was the daylight. As the group of weary travelers made their way from the cars to their hotel rooms, Euell and Mandy visited with John and his family for a few minutes before going to the Lassiter's room. Both Dr. and Mrs. Lassiter were sitting before the television sleepily watching the news. Mandy and Euell sat off to one side of the room talking softly and half-heartedly glancing at the television occasionally.

By eleven-thirty it was apparent that Mandy's parents were fast asleep in front of the television set. So, Euell whispered, "I should go now and let you get some much deserved sleep."

"I guess you're right," she replied haltingly and sleepily.

"Walk me to the door?" Euell asked.

"Sure."

"It has been really great seeing everyone today. And, I hope I didn't bore everyone with the sightseeing and the stories," Euell said apologetically.

"Not at all. Well, maybe John's little sister. But, she will have plenty of opportunities for fun stuff while she is here."

Euell and Mandy gently embraced and kissed each other in a loving, brief moment before saying goodnight.

" Seven A.M. all right with you?" asked Euell.

"Perfectly all right," Mandy replied.

Chapter 35

The Picnic and the Future

The traveling group enjoyed many activities together. But, at other times, the Lassiters and the Eastons went their own way. Either way, they all enjoyed a wide array of activities including movie shows, plays, museums, concerts, bicycling, kayaking, go cart racing, dining, swimming, lounging around the pool, excursions to nearby communities and sites, miniature golf, long walks, river rafting, and reading. With so many activities the time passed all too quickly and the last full day was upon them.

The plans for an all-day picnic had been methodically worked out. The venue was the new park. The participants included the Lassiters, the Eastons, the Cunninghams, the Brightons, the Wilsons, various church members, a few students from the university and the Christian college, as well as staff and students from the youth center.

The picnic day started with a breakfast in the park. Everyone picked up something from a fast food establishment, and brought it to the park at 7 AM.

Pastor Wilson suggested starting the day with prayer. "Dear

Lord Jesus, we ask that you bless this food to the nourishment of our bodies and that you bless us and use us for your glory and your purpose. May today's activities begin a life long relationship among those who have gathered here today. May we find strength in each other to never abort the mission for which you created us. Bless each one according to your riches in glory. In Jesus' name, Amen."

Tables were quickly moved to accommodate the large gathering. Excited chatter accompanied the consumption of sacks of food from every known fast food establishment in town.

After breakfast the tables were cleared of all but ice chests full of lunch food. A random drawing determined who would play on each side of the softball game. Then individuals kind of selected their own playing positions. If someone was more experienced than another, he or she usually got the position after a brief meeting of the minds. Euell was the most logical choice for the pitcher of his team. Rules were discussed and everyone agreed that the pitcher's main job was to make certain that no one struck out. The goal was to give each batter the best shot at a hit and play the consequences out. This gave the infield and outfield more opportunities to really engage in the game.

Euell's opposing team was up to bat first. Sam Bartell, the youth center administrator, stepped up to the plate. The first pitch brought a strike. The next resulted in a solid hit to left field.

The basic scenario played out over and over as Euell would gauge the batter's first attempt and adjust the pitch for the batter's success. This method loaded the bases very quickly. The fourth batter hit a ground ball that was picked up in the infield and thrown to home base to prevent a home run.

Euell continued the strategy of using the first pitch as a throwaway toss. With this in mind, Euell gave the next batter a faster first pitch. He didn't expect a hit, and so he was caught completely off guard when the ball came back at him faster than it had left his hand. He tried to duck, turn, and catch the ball all at the same time. The ball had other ideas. It bounced off his forehead and Euell was down and out.

Mandy was among the first to reach Euell. "Are you all right?" she asked as she gently raised his head ever so slightly and bent closer to his face. "Euell! Please be all right!"

"He's coming to!" exclaimed someone in the crowd. Indeed, he was stirring around, blinking his eyes, and moving his head from side to side as he felt his forehead.

"I am really sorry," the batter said sincerely.

"It's not your fault. I just didn't duck fast enough. Besides, that was a solid hit. Well, actually two solid hits. The bat to ball first, and the ball to my head next."

Mrs. Cunningham brought a bag of ice and placed it on Euell's forehead. "Hold this in place for a while. I'll get you a towel so that your hand doesn't freeze."

The youth center personnel dealt with this kind of injury regularly. So they checked Euell's eye response to movement of an extraneous object as well as the dilation and constriction of both eyes as the light condition changed when Euell opened and closed his eyes on command.

"Everyone go ahead and play the game," Euell suggested. "I'll be all right after while."

The players reluctantly took to the field and continued where they had left off.

"Does that kind of thing happen to you very often?" Mandy asked.

"Not really. I mean, I've been hit on the leg, in the chest, and on the hip. This was the first time to have been hit on the head."

"I was really frightened. I can't imagine a world without you," Mandy said tearfully.

"It's all right, Mandy. I'll be fine. The game is kind of like life. None of us go through without injuries and scars. Without the pains we couldn't appreciate the pleasures."

The players kept looking toward the young shade trees under which Euell lay. Finally the pitcher yelled, "Euell, are you ready to get back into the game?"

To Mandy's surprise Euell said, "Sure, I'll give it another try."

For the first five or ten minutes back in the game Euell couldn't really concentrate, or control the ball very well. But, he gradually got back up to speed.

The game broke for a change of players. Not every one wanted to play. So some of the same players returned to the field, while others were new to the day's game. This didn't last too long. Someone suggested cutting the watermelons. An assembly line was formed for cutting the melons, placing them onto plates, providing a knife or spoon, and a small package or two of salt. No announcement was made to let the players in on the melon feast. It wasn't necessary. The players saw what was happening and gave up the game in favor of the melons.

The conversation was sparse as people ate and cooled off. Most had finished eating when Mandy made an announcement. "We should have introduced everyone earlier. But, better late than never. I would like for each of you to introduce yourself and tell a little about your life and goals."

Euell noticed the commonality. Most were Christians. Educational aspirations and accomplishments were everywhere evident. These were people with dreams, hopes, goals, and the tenacity to stay the course. And, they were genuinely nice, decent, and gentle people. But, one thing that struck Euell was that until this day, he had not known the given names of his friend's wives. The one exception was Pastor Wilson's wife, Martha. Perhaps his mother's emotional distance and total disregard for Euell had made him subconsciously adverse to women. These were the guilty thoughts Euell was in the midst of when Mandy said, "Isn't it odd? I mean the fact that all the wives, as well as our mothers, and John's sister, have "M" names. There's my mother, Mindy, Melissa Easton, John's sister Michelle, your mother, Martha, Martha Wilson, Mavis Cunningham, and Mary Brighton. One of the youth group leaders is Monica."

"It is odd indeed," Mrs. Cunningham stated. "I mean, what are the chances?"

Euell spoke softly to Mandy and said that he had just realized something very important about his upbringing, attitudes toward women, and interaction with them. "I'll tell you about it later," he promised as the next event was announced.

One legged sack races, horseshoes, badminton, volleyball, basketball, and croquet were offered based on the number of interested people. Individuals made their choices and switched from one to another activity at will and as the opportunity presented itself.

Those preparing the barbecue and fixing other foods announced that lunch would be ready in ten minutes. This gave everyone a chance to get cleaned up and situated for the feast.

The food and friendship was everything that Euell had missed as a child. Maybe that's why he had enjoyed the day so much. No one had acted in a domineering, rude, or selfish way all day. The people seemed to genuinely enjoy each other's company. New friendships were being made. Perhaps this was a glimpse of heaven.

After lunch people kind of lounged around, or took walks, or sat and talked under the trees. In the presence of a number of Euell's friends, Mrs. Brighton asked Euell who his inspiration was when he was younger. This was an easy question to answer. It had to be the uncle who had bought him the clothes when he was being picked on in school.

"My mother's much older brother was my real hero and friend. He introduced me to fifties and early-sixties rock 'n' roll music, bought me clothes when I had almost none, gave me some sense of worth, and taught me that I needed to be a fighter in life. I remember a funny story he told me. He was really into street rods and early Corvettes. His first Corvette was a 1960 model. It had a 283 engine and a powerglide transmission. One of his friends kept asking him to race. He always said no. But, one night, in a weak moment, he consented. The Corvette was up against a Dodge 318. The highway selected had no on or off ramps for almost half a mile. At the traffic light, the two cars lined up and raced toward the first exit. It was a dead heat. So the race was run a second time. This time, before they could reach the off ramp, another car was gaining on them. My uncle and the other guy thought that it was surely a cop. It turns out that it was a brand new 1965 GTO, and the driver wanted both cars out of his way. My uncle learned that night, that his car wasn't the fastest thing in town. But, three years later he owned a year old 1967 Corvette Stingray fastback, with a four hundred horsepower 427 engine, four on the floor transmission, and three two barrel carburetors. He and his wife took a drive to a small town in the southern San Joaquin Valley of California. They stopped at a drive-in and felt uncomfortable because the people seemed to watching them strangely. This prompted my uncle to leave before even ordering anything. As he and his wife pulled out of the parking lot, a hot Mustang and another car followed them toward a stretch of road that led to another small community not far away. When it appeared that the Mustang driver was about to do something, like run them off the road, he down shifted and hit the accelerator for the three deuces to kick in fully. The Stingray lurched forward and left the other two cars far behind. When he and his wife reached the next town they sat in a hamburger stand parking lot eating and discussing the reason for the car chase. When my uncle got out of the car for something, he noticed that he had failed to take the for sale sign out of the rear window of the car. The poor guys he had out accelerated probably only wanted to inquire about the asking price of the car. His wife never let him live it down." Those within hearing distance got a kick out of the story, even though they were not really "car people" as such.

The time finally came for Euell and Mandy to lead the karate class from the youth center in a demonstration of the various aspects of the martial art. They and the class members changed clothes in the rest rooms. The crowd watched as they lined up and went through their opening rituals. As the demonstration continued, the crowd watched with varying degrees of interest until the sparring segment. When Euell had the students line up in sparring formation most everyone began to pay attention. The competition proved to be a crowd pleaser. This was especially the case when Euell, Mandy, and John alternatively sparred each other.

"Everyone listen up!" Euell said loudly. "It's time to get everybody involved."

There was some reluctance on the part of a large segment of the crowd. No one wanted to be embarrassed or to be in a new, awkward situation. Finally, after much coaxing, most everyone was coming forward. Euell demonstrated a particular technique and its proper execution. The class was in front of the crowd as a template or example. John and Mandy walked through the crowd correcting stances and techniques. When it was over, Dr. Cunningham confided in Euell. "If I were a little younger, and a great deal more flexible, I would consider joining a karate class. But, I have to confess, I even embarrassed myself with my awkward attempts to imitate your example."

"Well, I saw you, Dr. Cunningham. You were doing fine. But, karate is like most everything else. It takes a lot of practice and patience."

Music was next on the agenda. Euell opened his cases and brought out his guitar and saxophone. As it turned out, Mr. Brighton was a very accomplished guitarist and agreed to back Euell on the guitar while Euell played the sax. For thirty minutes or more, the two friends played music and the crowd thoroughly enjoyed the concert. Mary Brighton suggested that her husband make a fast trip home for his guitar. He agreed immediately. Upon his return, he and Euell went off from the crowd for a quick practice session. They returned ready for a sing along. Some in the crowd were good singers. Others were not especially gifted in this area. But, all of them seemed to have a good time. The music capped off a fantastic day.

As the friends picked up their things, they wished the Lassiters and Eastons a safe flight for the next day, and expressed a desire to do another picnic in the near future.

When Mandy and Euell arrived at the hotel they were filled with mixed emotions. There had been fun moments, memories made, and friendships established or strengthened. Everyone was tired beyond all endurance. But, Mandy and Euell had not been alone much of the day. They took a walk and spoke of things foremost on their minds.

"Instead of going back with your parents, let's get married tomorrow," Euell suggested.

"I would love to. But, we have so many things to seriously consider. Things like college, jobs, and future plans. And, my parents and our friends would be terribly upset and disappointed if we didn't include them."

"I know. It's just that I will be back to the grind the day after tomorrow and I will be alone again, without you."

"You won't be *all* alone. I'll be with you in my thoughts and prayers. And, your good friends will be here with you."

"You're right, of course. But, I'm missing you already. Let's make some definite plans tomorrow for all our tomorrows. I know that it's time to make the important decisions."

Alvis West

Mandy spoke confidently and sincerely when she said, "I know that I can not live without you. We were destined for each other. But, it is all in God's hands."

Chapter 36

Alpha and Omega

Much of what we call life is anything but what it seems on the surface. Smoke, shadows, and potentialities occlude the clear vision for clarity of thought and for reality itself.

At this juncture, we need to take a hard look back in time and analyze a little over nineteen years of one life. That of Euell Edwards. He seemingly developed into a unique, lovable, kind, considerate, honest, hardworking, moral human being despite the less than desirable situation at home. He influenced others for the ultimate good. Lives were changed by this one life. Mandy was spared serious injury, disability or death, as well as a life of loneliness. John had a genuine friend he could depend on, who led him to Christ and eternal salvation, and who helped make life worthwhile. Frank's life was spared by Euell's physical intervention on behalf of both himself and Frank when gang members intended to protect their turf from intrusion. And, Frank learned how to relate to people, gave up his bully-boy behavior, made a career for himself, helped Martha Edwards survive, and through his compassionate aid for Mrs. Edwards, allowed Euell to stay in college.

Pastor Wilson was influenced sufficiently to enroll in seminary in order to work toward a Ph.D. Young people from the youth center were influenced by a godly young man while at the same time learning softball, karate, self defense, saxophone, or guitar. The Cunninghams, Brightons, Wilsons, Eastons, Lassiters, church members from the church at home and in the new community, staff and students at the youth center, and fellow students and professors from both colleges, were befriended by Euell and changed by his example. Christian political activism had gotten a boost through Euell's dedicated efforts. A university was forced to look carefully at prejudice against people of faith. Euell's adult friends, including his uncle, had the joy of helping develop his character. As the angel, Clarence, observed in *It's a Wonderful Life*, "Strange, isn't it? Each man's life touches so many other lives, and when he isn't around he leaves an awful hole, doesn't he?" Now imagine for a moment all the lives touched by Euell, touching other lives. And, those lives touching yet other lives, ad infinitum. All of this begins with one life. One God-given life to be lived within God's perimeters and according to his purpose.

We know that God gives us free will. But, he also gives us direction for life in the Bible, and by his eternal presence. What God commands is part of his perfect will. What he presently allows is part of his permissive will. Free will and the fall of man postpone the perfect will of God until the end of the age and its eschatological fulfillment. Until then, one life, each life, will continue to influence the world.

The problem with the story of Euell Edwards is that it is not in reality, as it seems. Euell's mother was admitted to a facility one rainy night. She was prepped for a procedure that the staff and doctors performed day after day as a routine part of their "professional" lives. The decisions made by Mrs. Edwards were about to be carried to reality.

There was the sound of nurses preparing the surgical implements and talking about their personal lives and relationships interspersed with moments of professional banter. The doctor entered the room and quickly did a visual of the implements, machines, and staff before speaking with the patient.

"Well, Mrs. Edwards, are you ready for the magical moment?"

"I certainly am!"

"Well, nurses, let's make my next Farrari payment," he said, half jokingly.

"And the house payment too!" the head nurse said laughingly.

A very short period of time was all that was required. The silent scream was silenced forever. The procedure and a seared conscience were all that was required for Euell to never experience life outside the womb. The abortion ended at precisely eleven fifty-nine and fifty-nine seconds. The doctor had made one more baby-kill before high noon.

May Euell Edwards forever be the memorial to those who have known the womb, but never the breath of life.